The Enemy Held Near

Armand Rosamilia

and

Jay Wilburn

DevilDog Press

Editor: Jenny Adams
Cover art: Dane at ebooklaunch.com

Chapter 1
Foster Turner

I WAS CRYING too by the time I got Heather back home.

Heather took three steps into the house and stopped. Her duffle dangled by the straps in her fist, just a few inches off the floor, but she wouldn't release it. I stared at my daughter's back, but, without seeing her face, I couldn't get a perfect read on her emotions. She was twelve and she was female; I was never going to know what she was thinking or feeling even if I asked. I had fought to get her back home after she was taken and I was having mixed emotions. She had just been pulled out of her mother's arms by men with guns. As far as she was concerned, I was the one that sent the men and the guns. How could I expect her to have her head on straight?

Her eyes had been ringed red and raw before she walked in the door. Her muscles were tight like coiled springs now. I pushed the front door closed and only after I had done it did I realize I was afraid she would try to bolt. Heather's bag was already packed and she had been living on the run a couple weeks – going on three. And there was no telling what Ruthie had said to Heather about me before they fled.

I licked my lips and swallowed. It was a creepy

habit, but it was what I did when I was nervous. These girls had me nervous in my own house. Everything had me nervous.

I had no idea what to say to Heather to make it better anymore than I knew what to say to my wife. Still, I got my mouth and throat ready for whatever nonsense I was going to come up with that would inevitably make it all worse. I realized in that moment, with Heather's hair down and damp from the rain, how much she looked like Ruthie. That was not helping me come up with something to say.

Something clunked on a table deeper in the house and my throat went dry again.

Not now. Please, not now. I was barely holding shit together as it was. No time for this now.

It was a sound of something dropping or being pushed with force. It was the double sound of two impacts. It might have been a book dropping on its spine and then falling on its side. It could have been a knife coming down on the hilt and then falling to the flat of the blade. I couldn't stop picturing the knife. I thought I got all the knives out of the house, but there always seemed to be one or two more somewhere any time I looked – usually upstairs – the last place I wanted to find them.

I couldn't tell how deep in the house it had been. My eyes flicked to the darkness up the stairs and I waited for what might come next. The darkness and I were longtime roommates, but weren't friends anymore.

Sometimes people grow apart. Right?

Heather's shoulders tightened and I felt bad about bringing her back here. She was looking up the stairs

—

4

too. The darkness had not been good to her. Maybe not Ruthie either.

Maybe I was bad for them too. We should have handled this without the men with guns. I was not going to be able to hold together the act of being normal long enough. The women in my life were not going to allow it.

At first, I took the silence to mean that the house didn't know what to say either. The old place was just clearing its throat. It was three floors and an attic of old dry wood and old furniture. We made it nervous and sometimes the place had to lick its lips just in case it thought of something to say. It was an old house with creepy habits.

Then, I heard the footsteps. They were drawing closer. It was downstairs with us. I left the house alone to go retrieve Heather from Child Protective Services. We met at a rendezvous point at a gas station where rainwater was pouring over the cover like a waterfall. They did not want me there when they took Heather from her mother. While we were playing these games, whatever craziness had come off of Ruthie was now downstairs with us.

Why now?

A voice joined the footsteps. "Are you happy with yourself?"

I was full of ice water and my heart was having a hell of a time trying to pump it around my veins. Sometimes I wished my heart would just give up trying and let the works go still. That was the Turner family retirement plan after all.

A shadow wavered from the kitchen across the floor into the foyer.

Maggie stepped out and stared at Heather and me. I actually would have rather faced a monster.

I blinked and shook my head to try to rattle out the loose bolts and irrational fear rolling around my skull. "You're not supposed to be here."

Maggie shrugged and rolled her eyes in the way that only fourteen year old girls could do to make their fathers feel like assholes. "Katie's family was having dinner. They offered to let me eat with them, but I didn't want to feel like a charity case. My life is sad enough already. So, I came home."

I gritted my teeth. "If anyone asks, you need to tell them you were at your friend's house like you were supposed to be and not here by yourself."

Maggie narrowed her eyes. "Anyone? Like a social worker, you mean? The one that will decide if we should live with mom or with you? Is that what you mean by anyone, Dad?"

After I had to quit football and then started getting fat, Maggie was the kind of girl that would have picked on me. It wasn't fair for me to put my baggage on her for shit I went through before she was born, but that's what I saw when she pulled out the sharp blade of her wit and sarcasm.

Damn, I thought I got rid of all the knives, but here's another one coming right at me off my fourteen year old daughter's tongue.

"Just do what I tell you to do while we work out the adult stuff again," I said. My throat tightened. I fought the urge to lick my lips. My older daughter would point out that it was creepy and I'd just be more self conscious and nervous.

The words felt heavy in my mouth. I was

—

6

occupying a space outside myself, choosing every word and even the tone of the words like someone was listening. I was speaking with the thought that everything I said now was going to be repeated as decisions were made about my life, by people outside of my life.

There was never a better house for out of body experiences in all of Atlanta.

"If you're worried about what people will think," Maggie said, swiping red dyed hair from her face, "then you should fix us something to eat like real families do."

Maggie wanted me to notice that she had dyed her hair a few shades past natural. A little more red dye would have made it purple. She probably did it because I had told her not to more than because she wanted to. If I pretended not to notice, she would come up with something else to test me. If I called her out on it, we would have the fight now that would be about everything except red hair. The women in my life had me on the ropes and I wasn't up for the next round yet.

My eyes went to the stairs and then the light from the kitchen. Maggie was watching my eyes. Someone in this house was always watching.

I said, "I'll put together something in a minute."

Maggie took her hand away from her hair and crossed her arms over her chest. Now she looked remarkably like Ruthie despite the over reddened hair. My wife possessed every person and every corner of the house even though she tried to get away. If Maggie had not been off with friends refusing to answer her phone, Ruthie would have taken her too.

I imagined my wife standing at the door with Heather and the hastily packed bags trying to decide whether to leave with just Heather or to abort the escape until Maggie was back in the pocket. In the desperate weeks that followed, I saw it in Maggie's face that she wished she had answered her mother's texts that day.

I imagined Ruthie doing lots of things now that she was away and it was eating me up inside.

Maggie gave another verbal jab. She was trying to soften me up with body blows. She wanted her father to drop his guard and expose his chin so that she could do some real damage. She wanted to mess up my face. This fight was personal, between old rivals. "If you are worried about Child Services, you should probably clean upstairs."

Damn, she's going for the chin anyway, I thought.

I looked up the stairs and I knew Maggie had seen it. It was time to throw in the towel.

I said, "Did you go upstairs?"

"Wouldn't dream of it, Dad."

"I'll clean up soon. Thank you for the reminder."

Maggie opened her mouth for her next swing, but Heather dropped her bag and let out a sob that echoed through the house. My chest tightened with fear. She charged forward and slammed into her sister, wrapping her up in a hug that pinned Maggie's arms to her side. Maggie staggered backward. Her eyes went wide as she looked through her sister's hair that was still natural blondish brown like their mother.

The ref should really break this up.

Maggie pulled her arms free of her younger sister's grip and took hold of Heather as she cried into

—

Maggie's shoulder and dye job.

I reached back and locked the deadbolt behind me before walking past the girls to the kitchen.

I opened the freezer and stared through the fog at mini corn cobs in a bag and broccoli florets held by a pink chip clip. These vegetables were only there because Ruthie bought them before she left a few weeks ago. I wondered if Heather ate vegetables even when she was on the run while I fed Maggie fast food most nights at home.

Let me explain, your honor, I thought to myself. Then, my head went empty ... I got nothing, sir.

I took out the folded up bag of diced chicken. The bag was emerald green and had a picture of a family laughing as they enjoyed dinner together. I turned it so that I was looking at the heating instructions side. Why was the chicken company messing with me? I pulled apart the resealable ziplock and stared in at two rocks of chicken bound together in frost.

I brought the bag to the stove and turned on the bulb above the elements with a pop. I opened the cabinet. I considered between the box macaroni and box Rice-a-Roni as if it was being discussed at a hearing.

And what did he fix you for dinner the night he left you two crying in the foyer?

I took down the fried rice. We were out of butter, so I poured vegetable oil into the pan and turned on the element. The side of the bottle still had black grease smeared from the last time I used the vegetable oil to coat the charcoal grill. Ruthie hated me getting black smut on things when I grilled. I couldn't remember the last time we had grilled.

—
9

I turned and spotted the knife blocks. They were mostly empty, but a few had been put back in place. Put back for whom? I wondered. As I put the oil back in the cabinet, I saw a bottle of Jack Daniels. We didn't keep alcohol in the house, even for cooking, because of Ruthie's past. Did I buy it? I couldn't remember. I needed to get rid of it before the inspection happened.

I pulled it down and uncapped it. I poured the half empty bottle down the sink. Why was it half empty? I listened over my shoulders for the girls. I didn't want them to see this.

I heard the girls whispering in the next room. Even at their worst, they had always been tight co-conspirators against me and Ruthie. They were the united front of the family as mom and dad were at odds. I felt a lump in my throat as I thought about the girls being separated for this long.

I found the energy and will to blame Ruthie for it. She left. She split them up. I was only going to fall on so many swords before this ritual was going to get old.

"Where is she?"

"She's in some trailer. I don't remember the name of the town, but it's close. They made her come back."

"Where did you go?"

"Lots of places."

I capped the bottle and dropped it in the trash under the sink. I made a mental note to take out the trash sooner than later.

I returned to the stove. I dropped in the two ice balls of chicken and the oil spit and hissed. I

---

whispered, "Don't you start with me, too."

I looked down on the floor. Crumbs gathered in the corners. The molding separated at dark edges where the old house had settled over the decades. Houses this old had the biggest, fattest molding along the floor and ceiling that showed every stain and scuff. I saw two dried mushrooms shriveled just below the stove. I didn't remember the last time I had cooked mushrooms. Someone must have been sneaking them in with the alcohol. I was suffering from food amnesia. Maybe this was why the kids took pictures of food when they ate. There was a torn corner of a dried food pouch cast aside as well. I picked that up and made a note to sweep before the home visit.

I wondered if it was an announced visit or not. I had been told, but couldn't remember. I should have taken a selfie. I decided I better sweep soon.

I poured the dried rice, into the oil, on top of the thawing chicken.

"It's been awful ... worse than usual."

"Maybe they will be nicer when they aren't around each other."

"Not so far that I can tell."

I cleared my throat and stepped away from the stove. Gloves back on. "Maggie, let me see you a minute."

I heard the huff. It came from the endless well of frustration within the soul of my fourteen year old and it could be heard from the next room.

She stepped into the archway. Her arms were crossed. "What?"

"Set the table, please."

Maggie tilted her head and I braced myself as I stepped back to the stove and stirred the chicken and rice. Maggie said, "Just three for dinner tonight?"

Oh, shit, that was good. That was a pro level shot. It was layered and had depth. It was almost poetry.

"Maggie." I took a couple deep breaths. I poured in a cup of water and covered the pan with a lid that was too big. "Be part of the solution, not part of the problem."

She bowed her head and tears erupted. She moved to the cabinets and started pulling plates and cups.

I felt hollow inside. There was nothing poetic about making my daughter cry. Foster Turner was out of the running for father of the year once again. I was always a dark horse candidate at best.

There was a clunk on a table like before in the same double hit pattern. It was definitely upstairs, almost directly overhead. I looked up at the ceiling, trying to convince myself that it was related to Maggie shuffling in the cabinets.

There was a crackle that traveled diagonally through one of the floors above. It was a change in pressure like one of the doors being opened.

"Where is your sister?"

"She laid down in her room to rest." Maggie slammed a cabinet. That was a different noise from the clunk above. "I told her I would wake her up when the feast was ready."

I shook my head. "I heard you talking before I called you."

"I don't know what you heard, but she has been lying down since you started cooking."

"Downstairs?"

Maggie cleared her throat. "That's where we eat, sleep, live, and suffer."

She walked past with the dishes and cups.

I turned the heat to low and walked out of the kitchen into the foyer. Standing at the bottom of the stairs, I felt wind on my face. It was cold like a window had been left open. Someone would have had to have gone up for a window to be open. I had not even been up to sort my collections in the second floor rooms for days.

There was wind on my face.

I lifted a foot to the first step to go check. The roommate needed some attention.

I heard a car horn echo through the space around me and water dripped from the ceiling into puddles on the concrete floor. It made me think about being back at the gas station waiting for them to bring Heather. I felt sharp bits of grit bite into my bare feet and I looked down at my feet in the darkness to try to figure out what happened to my shoes.

I was only wearing my sagging boxers. It was the pair I put on for sleeping.

I raised my head to see the abandoned warehouse around me.

It wouldn't fade; the cold of the wind and the smell of piss rose from the trash around me with the hard edge of reality. I remembered carrying Ruthie years ago. I forced the memory out so I could deal with the present.

I turned and moved toward the closest opening where rain fell hard through the glow of streetlights outside.

I chose my steps carefully to avoid the spills of

broken glass.

Outside, I could see headlights through the thick trees beyond the other darkened buildings. Past the white dots of the rapidly moving headlights, I saw three rows of angry, red taillights whipping by the other direction. That could have been Interstate 75. That was the closest major road to our neighborhood between Buckhead and Midtown in Atlanta. I couldn't see the green signs hanging over the highway because of the trees. Atlanta had more trees than any city I knew. It was like they built the damn place in the forest. A primal past still infected the DNA of the city.

I stepped out of the warehouse into the rain.

"Where?" I breathed.

Past the chain link, I saw the pale neon for a club called Top to Bottoms. Unfortunately, I knew where I was. The touching rules were a little loose there. It wasn't high class like the Cheetah Club. Fortunately, it was closer to home. Not real close though. I was going to have to cross a highway to get home. Not 75, but I was going to have to use one of the bridges.

"Why now?" I said out loud. "I won't be able to explain this shit to the men with guns and the women with clipboards."

Why do this to me again now? Have I not been through enough shit lately? I came up with no answers to these thoughts.

I looked back toward the club.

I could see if the strip club would let me use the phone in my boxers.

I swallowed. "They would definitely let Ruthie have the girls then."

14

Jesus, where are the girls? How the hell did I get all the way out here? Are they in the house alone? I still had no answers.

I looked around the concrete and found a tattered section of blue plastic tarp. It smelled rotten as I wrapped up in it, but I shuffled barefoot along the asphalt behind the warehouse and out to the road.

I oriented from the club and the interstate. I followed the road north by northwest.

I moved farther off the road when headlights passed. After an hour, blue and red lights flashed on the street ahead. I stepped off into the alcove outside a dentist's office that I knew. I was close to home now. Still needed to cross the smaller highway, but I knew where to do it. Still, I waited for the lights of the cop car to decide to move on.

I looked up at the security camera over my head and then turned my face away. "Shit, I think Katie's dad works here."

Shivers from the damp cold seemed to have reached my bones. I was crying again.

I made it across the bridge, feeling exposed each time I passed under lights.

I kept my head down as I crossed the last intersection. The street light was out. There were bare foundations up the road before the houses on this side of the road started. I heard voices.

Our neighborhood was older, expensive homes. My parents had lived there and my father's parents too. The block before was like a different world with urban blight. We didn't let the girls walk or ride their bikes that direction. The houses that backed up to this street had higher fences across the back yards with wire across the top.

Once I crossed the intersection, I felt better. I kept my head down as I moved as quickly up the street as my bare feet would allow. My bad knee and back were starting to give me hell. Through the ache and cold, I was glad the rain was keeping our neighbors inside, but I wanted to be in before they called the cops.

I shed the tarp behind the hedges by the front door and used the key hidden under the fake rock to get back inside.

I looked at the stairs again. The house was dark. "Fuck you."

I ran through the house, dripping water on the hardwood, until I reached the girls' rooms. Both Heather and Maggie were in their beds asleep. Heather's bag was still packed at the foot of the bed. Her clock said it was 3:30 in the morning.

I slipped back out and looked at the dining room table. There were three settings and the plates were dirty. We'd eaten, all of us, but I didn't remember it.

I stepped into the kitchen and saw the pan in the sink, full of water and suds. That was my move too. Dinner and bed had occurred in the darkness between the stairs and the warehouse near the strip club.

I went to my room at the other end of the ground floor. The sheet and comforter were pulled down on my side. Ruthie's side, the wall side, was untouched. She had taken her pillow with her when she left. She never went anywhere without her pillow. We didn't take many trips as a family. "You're traveling alone now too, I guess, huh, Ruthie? Traveling alone again."

Maybe she had left that day in a blackout too, I thought. Don't mention the blackout during the visit. If you do, they won't care so much about the dried mushrooms on the floor. Maybe the empty bottle in the trash. I reminded myself to empty the trash again.

The shower hissed once turned on and I shed my soaked boxers. I could still smell the stink of whatever had been on the tarp.

In the dark, I stepped into the hot water and let it scald my skin. I bowed my head into the water and felt the cold water give way to hot through my hair.

Like thawing icy chicken balls.

I was staying fat, but my hair was getting thinner. Life was about trade offs. Sometimes you wake up in bed and sometimes you wake up nearly naked in a warehouse across town with missing time. Sometimes the wife stays and sometimes she abandons you, taking one daughter, but leaving the other to destroy the family.

I decided I was going to call into the realty company to let them know I would be in late. By the time I stepped out of the shower, the plan was modified to e-mailing that I wasn't coming in at all today. I was the boss after all.

Family business. It was the excuse that told nothing, but needed no explanation.

I rubbed at my face and hair with a towel that smelled almost as bad as the tarp. I thought about the girls waking up to find wet footprints across the floor. It would scare them. I needed to wipe those up before I went to bed.

I whispered, "I'm going to need to go upstairs sometime."

Chapter 2
Ruthie Sullivan Turner

IF I WAS being honest with myself, the bad choices were still impacting my life. The evil was still following me, covering my every move like a shadow no harsh direct light would make silent.

How did you go through your daily routine, as if nothing was happening? I'd watched the sappy dramas on television, where people were going through a traumatic event, but still found moments to smile and eat and sleep. I never understood it. I thought it was unrealistic.

Yet… here I was, cleaning the house of a rich couple in Lithia Springs. The husband was like Foster: married to his job and unable to just enjoy his family and the life he'd built. There was always another sale and another challenge. It didn't matter how much was in the bank or how many vacations we could take each year, or every other year, or the expensive cars and SUV's in the driveway.

Foster was going to do what he wanted like the stubborn mule he was.

This is not about Foster; this is about cleaning a house so I could buy groceries, I thought before dusting a vase worth more than my car.

I tried to think of anything but the family and my children and failed miserably.

What were Maggie and Heather doing right now? Were they safe in that house? Could Foster protect them, and would he at this point?

I saw enemies around every corner and wished things had been different. I sometimes wished my life had been different. What if my eighteenth birthday had gone differently? Down for death, across for hospital, as the saying goes.

The scars on my wrists were still there, faint unless you really looked. Angry pink lines that didn't suntan during the summer months. Foster knew they were there and now it felt like he'd reopened them with his teeth, trying to get to the blood and meat underneath.

As I dusted a picture of the happy rich family, with their two perfect children now grown and off saving the world, one as a doctor and one in the military, I couldn't help but wonder how badly we'd thrown our daughters off their paths. Had this mess pushed their trajectory so far askew they'd end up junkies or strippers or prostitutes?

I wanted to break the framed picture. Toss it on the expensive rug and step on it with my cheap sneakers and grind it into a million shards of glass, slicing the faces of the four perfect people.

It was raining outside, a perfect mirror to my mood. Just like it was the night they found me and took Heather. I didn't know why I'd bothered getting out of bed this morning, especially without Heather for the first time since the battle in the court.

—

I needed to speak with Maggie and explain why I'd left her behind. I was going to come back for her, but the house was too much to deal with, and I knew it wouldn't let me snatch both daughters from its gaping maw.

She hadn't looked at me during the hearing. Her own mother.

I knew Foster had also been shunned by both girls, but it gave me little comfort. Teenage girls - Heather would be there soon enough - needed their mothers for guidance. They needed the stability. They needed me. Foster also knew they needed to get out of his house.

His house.

It had been his parent's home, in their family forever. Even when we were married and I rearranged the furniture and put a fresh coat of paint on the walls, decorated with bright new curtains and we spent a summer building a deck out back and cleaning out fifty years worth of debris from the garage, it had always been Foster's home. A Turner monument to generations past.

We put the stuff from the garage on the curb, but that night I saw him bring the stuff off the pile back into the house and upstairs. As far as I knew, it was still up there. Everything taken out was eventually brought back in.

If I'd lived in the giant home for a hundred years, I'd still be an outsider and I knew it from the moment Foster had brought me inside off my own trash heap. The Turner blood had been spilled inside the home, literally and figuratively, and no matter what happened I'd be an enemy. I just hoped my daughters, who were tainted with Foster's DNA, would be spared.

"You alright?"

I turned, startled, to see an older man standing in the doorway to the kitchen. He was holding a martini glass and stirring it with a pinkie.

How had he come into the house without me knowing? Did he live here? Was he a nosy neighbor or friend of the family?

"Can I help you?" I asked, casually glancing around to find a weapon in case I needed it. In my younger, wilder days, when I was something to look at, I'd been attacked a few times. Nothing ever severe, but enough to almost keep me from my vices for a few weeks at a time. Guys that did that sort of thing sometimes had to work themselves up to it. They had creepy banter that they used to get close.

I hadn't felt this exposed and defenseless in years. Ever since Foster came along and pulled me from the gutter that was my life. The man had saved me from myself, and yet... I'd abandoned my marriage and life and sabotaged it all?

No. I'd done what needed to be done. I'd gotten out of the house before it killed me and I was trying to save my daughters before it was too late. Simple as that.

"Are you sure?" The man asked, taking a small step forward and putting the glass to his thin lips.

I knew him from somewhere, like a man I'd passed in the streets each day going or coming from work. Someone who played a tertiary role in my world, but until this moment we'd never spoken.

I didn't understand his question. I took three steps

to my right, hoping I could get out of the screen door before he attacked. I felt a rush of energy and emotion emanating from the man and knew he meant to do me harm. He had the banter and feel of a guy gearing up for it.

The martini glass was pulled from his lips and he held it in front of his eyes, staring into the half-empty liquid.

"The door is open. I won't hurt you here. You have my word. I only ask you to reconsider what you're doing," he said without looking at me.

"What am I doing?"

A chill ran up and down my arms and centered in my chest, threatening to freeze my organs and leave me to die. I felt such horror and shock from this man, who was so much more than a mere mortal. I just knew it.

"You need to go home. You need to make your marriage work for the sake of the children. Don't you want to keep them out of harm's way?"

I took a step forward, anger making me suddenly bold. No one threatened my girls.

"I'm going to call the police if you don't leave. Stay away from my family," I shouted.

He shrugged his broad shoulders and pursed his lips, the martini glass tilting slowly forward.

"You need to go home and make amends before it's too late," he said before dumping his drink on the expensive carpet.

I screamed, hoping a neighbor would hear the commotion.

He winked at me and smiled unpleasantly, knowing he'd somehow bested me in this clash of wills. He'd gotten into my head and I hated the man for it – the man I didn't know but knew I'd seen before.

My phone was in my purse behind him in the kitchen.

"I'm confident, in the end, you'll make the right choice, Ruthie."

He turned and walked into the kitchen and out of sight.

I wanted to rush and get my phone, but waited for the front door to open so I would know he'd left.

My heart was hammering and there wasn't a sound. Was he messing with me? Waiting behind the kitchen island or in the pantry to pounce?

The home didn't have a landline, an antiquated concept in this digital age. Foster had always kept the old rotary phone on the wall in the kitchen. The girls thought it was a prop or something old people hung on their walls for show, but it actually worked. Not that any of us would use it since we all had cell phones and standing in our kitchen with twelve feet of dangling cord to tether us to the wall wasn't much fun.

There were knives in the kitchen of the house I was cleaning. I needed something to protect me. I didn't want to die today, or any day.

It would be ironic if I came to my end in this giant mansion, surrounded by all of these expensive and gaudy artifacts the couple collected for me to dust. My corpse would rot on thousand dollar carpets and my blood would soak into the best wooden flooring underneath.

I'd imagined I was well past dying by another

person's hands by now.

How many nights in my younger days had I been woken, stoned and tired, in an alley, by a homeless man trying to rape me? A police officer, high as a kite himself, looking to make an example of another runaway. I'd lied, stolen and come close to killing myself, more times than I cared to remember, for drugs. Foster had saved me, but now...

Was the man sent by my husband to scare me into giving up the girls? I didn't think Foster was capable of such a heinous act, but then who knew what people were capable of when push came to shove.

I could count on both hands the number of people in my life that I'd trusted. People who waited until I dropped my guard and then took as much as they could from me, physically and mentally, before moving along to another mark and another sucker.

There was a gaudy ornate cross hanging on the wall of the living room, definitely a decoration and not a profession of religious beliefs. I'd been in this family's drawers and knew the kinky things the husband liked to watch. If he truly believed in God, he would've burned those videos and toys or never thought to purchase and hide them in his man cave under his manly sports magazine collection.

The wife was just as bad. She kept in touch with her old boyfriend from college, sending messages on the computer and mailing items back and forth. The collection of baubles and sexually explicit videos they'd exchanged made me blush, yet I couldn't stop watching sometimes and was ashamed.

I didn't believe I was doing anything wrong, although if I thought too hard and used common sense… no, I was trying to help them. Some videos would get erased, letters destroyed, and whenever the couple was together I made sure to interact with both and try to get them to share stories about happier days together. I never stole anything of value.

They were a broken couple, but I saw the love in their eyes, even if they thought they'd lost it. They just needed a gentle push in the right direction.

What about me and Foster? Could we fix this? Not if the house was still in the equation and a huge part of our lives.

I was stalling.

I hadn't heard the door open and close, but there was no sound coming from the kitchen. I took a step forward, glad the carpet was so thick. I moved to my right to get a better angle so he didn't surprise me.

My purse came into view, but it may as well have been a hundred miles away, past shark infested waters. If he was still in the house, he could easily be hidden in ten different corners of the kitchen.

"I've called the police," I shouted, the sound echoing through the home. "If you leave now, maybe you'll escape."

Two more steps closer but still no sound. I tried to reason with my fear: why would he confront me and then go into the kitchen and hide, so he could scare me again? He was physically imposing and could've easily killed or hurt me if he wanted. We were alone in the house.

I tried to think back to what he'd said.

I'm confident in the end you'll make the right choice, Ruthie.

There was no other choice to make but about my

---

children. Foster had sent this man to scare me into... giving up rights to the girls? Not wanting alimony? What?

The first phone call was going to be to 911 and the second to my lawyer. Foster couldn't scare me into submission.

Of all the lowdown dirty tricks...

I was in the kitchen and looked to be alone. I had been holding my breath and finally exhaled before dashing across the tiled floor, my footsteps like gunshots and imaginary hands grasping at me as I moved.

My hands, feeling like watermelons, swiped at the purse and knocked it over the center counter and onto the floor behind. I knew, just knew, the man was on the other side with a grin on his face and now waiting to pounce.

"I think I hear the police coming down the lane," I yelled.

I tried to will my hands to stop shaking. They hadn't moved so quickly since I'd kicked heroin for the last time. I hoped the last time. The twelve steps always made it clear you were one bad choice away from falling off the wagon and devolving back into a horrible life. Each day sober and clean was a gift from God. Each day was worth living... each day...

I rushed around the center counter island and stumbled, panicking when I thought I'd been duped and he was right behind the counter and he'd grabbed my heel and now he'd slam me to the ground and my head would hit the floor and I'd bleed out from a cracked skull head injury, the family in this giant lonely house not coming home for a week and...

I'd stepped on my lipstick.

The contents of my purse were on the floor and I grabbed my cell phone, about to dial 911 when I stopped. What would I tell the police? What if Foster had done this on purpose to not only spook me but to make me look crazy? I knew, if this got ugly, he'd use my past as a drug addict against me.

I kept the phone in one hand, ready to use, and pulled the biggest knife from the counter with the other. I made sure he wasn't still hiding in the kitchen, opening the pantry doors and even the fridge, feeling foolish.

When I went into the foyer, I saw the front door closed and locked from this side. Even the deadbolt was still engaged. The only way you did that from the outside was with the key. The family never used it, but I did automatically every time I entered. The home was too big to hear people walking in sometimes and I wanted to make sure I was doing my job and not going through their private things when someone came home unexpectedly.

Was he still inside the house? My gut feeling was he was long gone and I was alone, but I needed to check. I opened the nearest closet door and stared at the jumbled mess of dusty sweaters and jackets, a deflated basketball and a pair of ancient skis. This was the vacation closet, where dreams went to die. I could pull it apart and figure out where the last ten years of expensive and hollow trips had been. I'd seen some of the pictures around the house, fake smiles and faraway looks in their eyes.

I needed to concentrate and fix my problem before worrying about theirs.

An hour later I was done roaming through the house, making notes in my head to clean and dust as well as snoop into a few drawers and closets.

I searched the children's rooms, now monuments to trophies and outdated posters, preserved by their mother in case they ever felt the need to return and relive their teens, I guessed. More than likely mom's way of remembering better times before her children flew the coop and created their own miserable family dynamics.

On one of my first visits to the rooms, I'd uncovered a box of rolling papers. I still remembered the feeling of dread and excitement: what if there was a baggie of pot tucked under the mattress still? How would I do? Would my willpower crumble?

I never found any drugs. The parents didn't even bother storing anything heavier than aspirin in their sparse bathroom. I assumed they carried their anxiety pills and anti-everything tablets on their persons for ease of use.

The house was empty except for me, the lonely maid looking for a shadow and a test of my resolve to stay off of drugs. I'd worry about Foster and the implications that this had turned bad and not in my favor.

I decided a call to the lawyer would do more harm than good for my case. I saw the way she looked at me whenever I tried to explain myself, pursing her lips and twisting my words so I didn't seem so needy and lost.

My hands were still shaking when I got back to dusting the living room. I needed to take the long way home and not cruise through the bad neighborhood tonight to test my resolve, because I knew I'd fail miserably and never see my children again. I needed to find that spill on the carpet and clean that up too.

Chapter 3
Foster Turner

"SHE'D BE DEAD if it wasn't for me."

I said it out loud, but regretted it as soon as it left my lips. I was on the second floor of the house, so it wasn't quite as bad as tempting fate on the third level or in the attic, but still, I knew better. Talking about death on those floors was just stupid. I barely had the strength to bend my knees to climb the stairs. If I started stirring up my own fear, then I wasn't going to make it long. I'd close my eyes in the trophy room and wake up half naked on the other side of town again.

The upper floors smelled like the pungent leafy odor from when my dad used to take me hunting in south Georgia. It was far enough south that we left roads behind and walked down into knee deep water that might as well have been Florida. I always expected to be eaten by an alligator. This was before the pythons took over the swamps, thank God. Now the smell reminded me of my parents' blood.

The sound of my words got absorbed into the spongy wood and peeling silk paper on the walls. It was swallowed by the furry things on the other side of the room with their mouths open. The house consumed my pronouncement about death and would use it against me eventually.

I faced the metal shelves and looked over the acrylic cases full of signed footballs, baseballs, bats, and cards. These did not speak of responsible spending. Other than dusting, there was not much to be done here. Child services was not going to take the girls because I failed to dust.

I looked over the peeling walls. That might do it. I could tear the loose bits off, but it wouldn't be much better. Full restoration was expensive, but not entirely out of reach if I wasn't hung up on perfect or original.

I turned and looked across the room at the animal trophies stacked on the other side. Elk, deer, bear, large cats, and moose heads sat on their mount boards along the floor as if their spirits were in the midst of ripping through the wood to escape into the real world. Their maws hung open with fangs out to show action, but sitting side by side along the floor like that, they appeared to be tortured and trapped between worlds. Most of them had died long before I was born.

"Killed," I said. "They were killed."

Damn it. What was I thinking? I did it again and the animal spirits swallowed my cursed sound once more.

Among the decapitated animals were whole zebras and kudu cows. What was I supposed to do with this? This might not be a technical violation with child services, but it was sure to leave an impression. I could move them to another floor, but they would just be piled with other furniture under dusty sheets and tarps for the visitors to find. Hanging them back on the walls might be the only way to get by. That would take pros too. Some of them weighed three hundred pounds or more.

Ruthie hated these damn things and now I was with her.

I stepped into the doorway and looked out along the banisters and wooden floors with tiny separations between the aging boards. The only thing keeping this from being an abandoned house was the pesky family that insisted on living on the ground floor.

I insisted, I thought. I'm the one that makes us live here.

"Well, I'm not the only one, am I?"

I waited for someone to answer – maybe the house itself. Thank God no one did answer or I would have wet my pants on the spot. The girls were at school, but if they decided to skip one day, they could hide up here and almost be guaranteed to not be found. Even if I heard them talking or walking around, I might not investigate. I think Maggie knew that and she had to have thought about using that against me at some point.

I stepped out of the trophy room and walked along the creaking floor. I followed the banister without looking down the drop and made the elbow turn. I went three closed doors down and stopped with my hand on a crystalline knob. If money ever got tight, we could probably sell the door knobs and be able to get by. The house wouldn't like it and there would be punishment. Maybe we could buy bus tickets with the money and just go away like Ruthie had wanted.

It was in that moment with my hand on the crystalline knob that I realized I hadn't really saved Ruthie in any way that mattered. She had survived overdoses and attacks. She had survived outside while high when she was just a kid not much older than our girls. She had tried to kill herself and had survived that. I was here when she got clean, but would she have done that anyway with whomever? Was I special to that or was I just "guy that was there?" I did the whole supportive thing and cold sweats and cleaning up vomit. Some guys would have walked away. Did I do it just because she let me do things to her and I thought it would be more fun to bang someone clean? That's not how the recovery story was supposed to be told, but was that entirely untrue? If getting clean with me just attached her to me, then did I do anything that mattered if she just ran away one day because of me? If we are here now in this state of affairs, then no one was saved. None of it mattered.

"Fuck her. She left." My voice echoed off the hard wood of the doors and walls of the hallway. The house let that pronouncement go without eating the words. Did that mean the house accepted the curse or rejected it?

I turned the knob and it felt loose in my hand. If it came off in my fist, would the house think I did it on purpose to sell it like I had thought? I didn't want to find out. The questionable knob held and the latch finally popped out from the warped door frame. The door swung inward. Some of the doors were hinged on the outside and some on the inside. There seemed to be no logic as to why.

The first thing I noticed was that the mattress was spotted black on one corner. It needed to be thrown out. How many of the rooms were in this condition now? I looked up at the high ceiling for a wet spot. If it was a leak, this was the second floor, so it was coming through the slate roof, the modified attic/loft, the third floor, and then here. That would be disastrous. That would be the worst clean-up in the history of the house and that was saying a lot – a hell of a lot.

I looked to the walls. Nothing had been splattered in here. The mold on the mattress could be from anything. The entire house was moist most of the time. Some of the pipes were the original copper and probably slime green in color in the walls and ceiling. Once those busted, the whole house might come down on itself. That's usually how these things end, isn't it?

I brought my eyes back to the mattress. There could be something inside. These old things were not made in factories. They were sewn shut shortly after the wood on the beds got their final finish. The decay could be coming from the inside out. I could take one of those knives that shouldn't be on the top floor to open it up and see what was rotting in the guts. Those kinds of surgeries never went well. Black mold was the bad stuff. If only that was the only blackness in my life or in my family – in this place.

Boxes lined the walls along two sides and out into the unused room. A few were open on top showing hard faced dolls with soft cloth bodies. I found myself wondering what was in their stuffing. More potential for black mold.

The dolls don't need my help to stay alive. They just need me to keep the knives away and get them out of the environment prone to decay.

I opened one of the boxes on the taller stack closest to me. It was a set of the martini glasses. I felt a chill move through me. Like the black mold, the chill started from the inside and worked its way out. These glasses were encrusted with dust that had gotten wet and then dried out again. It was grime with trails through it like tiny snails had explored the surfaces. I couldn't tell if they had been washed since last time they had been used. I wondered if there was one or two sitting on surfaces in the other rooms. I pictured them with a forgotten swallow left in them that had gone solid like the bacteria bait in a Petri dish.

I started to think my best bet was to bring in a crew to tear out and rebuild. If child services found the bottom floor livable and the top floors covered in plastic and scaffolding, that would pass. That would be a home in progress. No one would fault a remodel as bad parenting. It would clean me out of my liquid cash. I'd probably need a building loan too, of course. My lawyer budget would be razor thin, but still sharp enough to deal with Ruthie. She was out in the wind with house worker wages to fight her legal battles on. If she told the right lies, she might get one of those battered women organizations to back her. If she played it up in court, all the money in the world might not be good enough to help the monster father defeat the poor victimized mother.

If I tore open the walls, it might work in some houses. Here? There might be more trouble than I could handle. There might be more than I could survive. No one would be here to hold me through my troubles and recovery.

I heard a cough out in the hallway and the fear exploded from my heart, out through my body, like a shock. My heart rhythm did not feel regulated as a result. Hit me again. Another cough and snort made my heartbeat throb in my head.

I turned to the door. It hung a quarter open giving me a narrow view into the hall and no bead on anything that could explain an empty house coughing. I shook my head and stepped out. What choice did I have? I'm the one that came upstairs.

I pulled the door another quarter turn and leaned out. He was standing there by the banister. It was a linen suit with blue pin stripes. The boat shoes were a shade off from the trim of his suit. His hair stood up in puffy curls like it never needed to be brushed, but should be.

"If you're back here," I said, "Does that mean it's all over?"

He leaned over the banister staring down into the first level. That bothered me. I didn't like that he was even interested in the bottom floor. If he was, then maybe the others were too.

"Nothing's changed, Foster. She's not worthy of the history of our family and she needs to not cause trouble by trying to move the newest generation out of the house. That's not how this works."

"How does it work?" I asked.

He straightened and walked toward me. I backed up until my spine connected with the doorframe of the moldy bedroom.

As he approached, he said, "I raised you after your parents died, smart ass. A little respect for that fact wouldn't kill you."

"Won't it?"

He snorted again and pointed. "You mind if I take that."

I looked down and saw I was holding one of the cloudy martini glasses. I cleared my throat. "It's dirty."

He took it from my grasp from underneath the bowl. "That's how I like 'em."

As he held it out to his side, I expected the thing to suddenly be full of drink like they always were when I was young. It remained empty and grimy.

"I don't know if I can get her back," I said.

"She'll be back."

"How could you know that?"

"I left you too and now I'm back," he said.

I swallowed several times. "I don't want …"

I couldn't find the end of my sentence.

"Get it together, Foster. You're causing trouble here. Family doesn't have to be peaceful or even happy, but it has to be together. Get your house in order."

I looked up at the ceiling and around the hallway. "I don't think I put it out of order and I'm not sure it wants to be fixed."

"You know what I mean, smart ass. Do you need to spend some time in your room by yourself to think about it?"

It wasn't my room downstairs he was talking about. It wasn't really my room upstairs either, but it became my room when my parents died in it. My uncle would leave me in there with the knob removed to think about things for a while. I was an adult now, but I didn't know whether I could fight him off. I'd probably black out in the room and wake-up somewhere else on the planet. The room would smell wet like every other room, but it wouldn't remind me of leaves.

"No." My voice was small again like when I was a kid.

My uncle nodded and turned away. "Check with me before throwing anything out."

He ran the base of the glass along the banister and continued down the hall. He turned at the end of the hall and took the stairs to the third floor.

"You're the only reason she's still alive." His voice sounded closer than the stairs. "Believe it."

I licked my lips. I knew I needed to go up there eventually, but for now I just wanted to get downstairs.

Chapter 4
Ruthie Turner

I FELT SAD when I stared at the dark building. The broken windows looked like gaping eyes and the steel door the mouth, my imagination filling it with sharp teeth that bit through a little bit of your soul every time you walked through the maw.

Abandon all hope ye who enter...

This building, dead center of the roughest neighborhood in Atlanta, had been more home to me than anywhere else. I'd spent countless nights, days and long weekends high and dirty in this dilapidated crack house. I'm sure if I was able to count up the hours here against hours spent anywhere else in my life this four-story building, with piles of debris jammed between the worn bricks and cardboard covering some of the windows, would win out. Some places were more haunted than others.

Why am I here?

I'd been scared by the man in the house, but knew it was another excuse to fall off the wagon and get high. I needed a fix and it didn't matter what I got into my system right now.

Always an excuse to use again.

I didn't get out of my car. I'd fought the urge to drive downtown through the traffic, but, in the end, here I was, parked across the street and watching for signs of life. I didn't know if someone coming or going would mean anything, but I held my breath as if God giving me a sign to enter or flee was coming.

I wondered how long it had been since I'd used. I knew the general timeframe, but most people in rehab and at the meetings could give the number of days and down to the minute, if asked. Most even if you didn't ask.

I'm Billy, they'd say, and I've been clean for two thousand ninety eight days, fifty-seven minutes and fourteen seconds.

I'd been clean a long time. The girls had given me the strength to keep away from this side of town. I knew of other addicts who would do this drive each week or month as their ritual, to stare at the building they'd almost thrown their life away in and give it the finger. Tell it crack and meth had no control over them anymore. Laugh and drive away sober, as if it were so easy to do. Defy the ghosts. As if they weren't one bad day away from sucking on a glass pipe and letting strangers touch them, as long as they kept packing the pipe with heaven.

My hand was on the door handle. Was I seriously considering getting out of the car and crossing the street? I closed my eyes and took a deep breath, trying to remember a mantra or two from the meetings to help me through this.

I couldn't think of anything but the feeling of getting high. I hadn't done it in so long. Maybe it would feel like the first time again, the high you

—

spend the rest of your life chasing and never finding.

I willed myself to think of my daughters. They'd be gone to me, swallowed up inside the house of horrors with Foster. They'd never see the light of day. I'd never see the light of day, if I got out of this car and stepped inside Hell.

I needed to think of my children. Anything to put my fingers away from the door handle, which I realized I was softly stroking, as if my bad side of the brain was trying to coax my hand to do what it wanted.

"Heather and Maggie," I said to my disheveled face in the rearview mirror. I needed to focus on my girls. I had a daunting task ahead of me in court and getting high wouldn't be the answer. I knew if I broke down and was weak once I'd do it more and more. One misstep is all it took to lose days and weeks.

When I was just a little girl, I saw a drunken man make a sloppy pass at my mother outside of a bar, and it never left me. It took me years to realize what the most troubling aspect of the scene was and why it lingered: my mother had taken a six-year old to a bar and gave me two old dolls to amuse myself at a side table while she drank. My mind had always focused on the mean drunk hanging on her, trying to rub her back and touch her shoulders and more intimate places while the rest of the crowd sat and watched, bored, as if this was the norm. I knew now it was.

How many times had I been at the same table trying to keep myself amused while she drank herself into a stupor? I closed my eyes and remembered the pattern of the rings on the split wooden table. I still remembered tracing them with a small finger.

I opened my eyes and smiled as my hand moved on the dashboard in a knowing pattern. Muscle memory, I supposed.

Therapy and group sessions had brought out the real issues: I hated my slut mother and cheating father. I hated being a child in an adult world, forced to grow up too soon. Drugs and drink were my coping mechanisms. Smoking pot as a teenager wasn't to be rebellious. I had no one who cared enough about me to rebel against.

I did it to forget about my sorry life and what I would eventually become. I always saw myself sitting on the same stool as my mother had, with her short skirts and unbuttoned tops, waiting for the next drunk to buy her a drink so she could forget.

Foster had saved me, right?

He'd loved the younger, wilder me. The drunk chick that took crazy chances and was a borderline nymphomaniac in the beginning. He was so reserved. So vanilla to my chocolate, strawberry, and rum raisin with whipped cream and a cherry on top. I made him laugh and Foster made me feel safe. He made me almost want to stop using.

The house was calling my name as I sat there, waiting to either get the nerve to leave or have a random patrol car stop and question me. If they took my name and license plate, would I end up in a police report? Another black smudge Foster could use against me.

The man who'd threatened me wasn't someone I knew. Maybe someone I'd seen before, but never had a direct conversation with as far as I could tell.

I kept spinning all these random thoughts through

my head, as if they were a thousand piece jigsaw puzzle and only by connecting them together would the picture make sense.

The stranger. The drugs. My daughters. Foster. Money. The house.

The house.

I didn't know if I still believed in a Biblical God, the man with the white beard and even whiter robes who stood and watched us from above.. When I was fifteen and my mother stopped even bothering to come home to change out of her ragged clothes, I found myself in a church. I don't even remember where it was and I've never been back since. It was empty, a storm having ravaged the grounds and punched a hole in the roof the size of a mattress.

Rain had destroyed the dais, the floors slick with slime and a rotting moldy smell I will never forget. I snuck in through the shattered side door. I wanted to steal something, maybe. I don't remember now. I do remember seeing Jesus on the cross and a single candle, still lit, despite the breeze from the hole and the wetness in the church.

Did I find God that day? I sometimes think so. He didn't blind me with a ray of sunshine and his only son didn't step down off the cross and speak into my soul. There wasn't a brilliant epiphany, but I still think that day was a small change for me. I imagine it was the day before I started using drugs and drinking - even though it wasn't - and I could step back in time, reset to that moment and be myself again.

Foster had been my guiding light until he'd moved me into the house. I know I can pinpoint when it all went downhill: the first time I saw the hulking structure, like an alien edifice out of a movie. It was dark and imposing and cast such a wide shadow some parts of the lawn would never grow anything but weeds.

I'd been fine before we moved into the house. I acted like nothing was off and that having children running around on the wooden floors and hanging some drapes would brighten the gloomy structure up so the shadows and dark spots would retreat back upstairs and leave our family alone.

I was clean and sober, too. Never thought about scoring or doing bad things to get what I yearned for. Until the house started talking to me. Until…

Stop this.

I started the car, proud of myself for doing something positive. I needed to clear my head, go for a drive and stop at a Waffle House or the Varsity or another fast food restaurant and have something to eat and worry about the next day's work.

Don't look at the crack house I kept telling myself, but when I put the car in drive and turned my head to see if there was any traffic coming down the road, I looked.

I saw… something, standing in the shadows of the doorway watching me. I knew it was a man. A strong male, who'd been watching me, for the last few minutes, while I was deep in thought about a past that had no room in my life right now.

The past will come back to haunt you. I vaguely remembered a Bob Dylan line Foster used to sing back in the day, when he'd smoked an occasional roach and dreamed of his sorry college – Foster who had wasted four years. Foster would drink a beer every now and then and reminisce about what life could've been for both of us, but it was really just about his own broken dreams. He stopped keeping the beers in the house though. Most ballplayers could blame it on a bum knee. Foster just had a shit family and now a gut.

When you glorify the past, the future dries up... something along those lines.

I wondered how much danger I would've been in if I'd opened the door and walked across the street. Harm would come to me multiple ways, I was sure of it. If the drugs didn't kill me with an overdose, the watching figure would have. I wondered if it was Death or Jesus watching to see which path I took tonight, and if he'd stand guard in this doorway each and every night if I returned to tempt fate and stare my demons in the face. Jesus needed to do a better job of fixing his roofs and leave me alone.

Tomorrow was another day and I hoped I would be stronger. I'd stayed in the car, which was a small victory. The bigger victory would come when I stopped thinking about getting high and how it would magically solve all of my problems.

I needed to be strong for the girls, and for my soul.

Whether it was the Devil or an angel across the street no longer mattered. The job was done and I was driving away, back to my hovel after finding a cheap and quick meal to eat alone.

Chapter 5
MeLinda Goshen

I PULLED AT the screen door on the trailer and the hinges screamed. I braced it open with my shoulder, turning my fractured left arm in the sling away. I tapped the knuckles of my good hand against the marbled surface again.

I wasn't confident she would answer this time anymore than the previous two knocks. The trailer was dark and we had heard nothing inside. The concrete parking pad was empty. But sometimes they hid inside hoping we would go away. If I gave the impression that I wasn't, sometimes they opened it. I thought she probably was not actually home.

I turned around and saw eyes watching me from the other trailers. A few men without shirts stared at me with arms crossed. They tried to look like they weren't flexing, but they were. They also stood so I could see their best tattoos. They were like cats arching their backs. The people here knew who I was and the social worker was the enemy. A few women grabbed their kids by the arms and hustled them away. If I didn't find the children I sought, maybe they thought this old witch would come for them next.

They might be hiding Ruthie Turner. Sometimes they did that too until we left. Ruthie was new here, so she was probably still an outsider and on her own. Women that fled were always on their own.

Drew opened the driver's door and stood up, looking at me over the roof of the car. It was a refurbished police car from a couple decades past that served as a department car. They were letting me use it since I was hurt. The only work that had been done on it since it had become a Department of Child Protective Services car was a shitty tan paint job.

Drew was interning with us and now he was assigned to driving me because of my arm. Gordon insisted it was for safety, but I think he wanted me to have a witness until things cooled off from the Walters case. A father breaks the social worker's arm during an extraction and ends up arrested. Now I have an escort. The police were there, so why didn't that count as witnesses that I wasn't at fault?

"Because no one likes the bitch that takes the kids," I whispered.

I wasn't even sure this was her address. This was just the address we had. If she ran off again, it would make my job easier. We might still have to take the Turner girls, depending on what I found at their house or what I found out about the father. I still had one arm left to give, if it came to that.

Drew asked, "Do you want to give her a call?"

He looked young. He almost looked too young to be in college much less have graduated. I kind of wanted to take him out for drinks just to check his ID. I did have a driver after all. It was the perfect time to start drinking on the job.

"No, I want to surprise her the first time," I said.

As some of the watchers grew bored with me and drifted away, I thought my chances of surprise were pretty much a bust. They might have called her to warn her to stay away. Sometimes they did that.

"I thought we didn't have to do an unannounced on this one," he said.

"We don't," I said.

He licked his lips and folded his arms over the roof of the car. His hair stood up mussed in a way that was only achieved through product. He was a little awkward, but had that new nerdy hotness that probably got him plenty of play in school.

"Do you want to wait some more?"

"No, we can head down to the Turner house so the whole day isn't a bust." I walked down the wooden steps and back toward the car. "I'll show you on the map."

"I have it in my phone," Drew said as he got back behind the wheel.

We pulled out along the circle of the park back onto the main road leaving another cluster of trailers in peace for now.

The phone between our seats said, "Turn right on Dell Avenue."

Drew said, "Maybe we have the wrong address. We should call and check."

"Maybe," I said. "Sometimes we do. Maybe she lives in a nice condo with a playground and nice high fences."

"Maybe." Drew turned right on Dell.

"In nine miles, turn left on the 133 Service Road

South."

I looked over at his profile. He was still nerdy sexy. He did not seem to have an understanding of the sarcasm of what I had just said. Maybe he didn't understand it was a joke or just didn't think it was funny. He was young. He might not get that there was never going to be a nice, safe condo.

I looked back forward.

My phone rang and I saw it was Gordon. I moved my thumb to hit the green answer button when Drew laid down on the brakes. My phone went into the floorboard. The tires screamed against the asphalt and blue smoke boiled up into the air.

I expected to be eating glass from the windshield and plastic from the dashboard since this lovely model was too old for airbags. I nearly threw up my heart and swallowed it down again when I saw that drugged out basic bitch staring at us through the windshield . Her hair wasn't long, but hung down wet and heavy around her face and shoulders. Her nightgown and robe looked wet and dark too. She had a real drenched dog on meth look about her.

Drew managed to stop inches from clipping out her legs with the grill of the Crown Victoria. She would have tumbled through the glass into the seat with us like when you hit a deer. The car rocked on its frame and rattled near the front right quarter panel where it sounded like a strut snapped from the sudden stop.

In the quiet that followed, the warbling vibration of the engine idled around us. Her wide, dark-ringed eyes held us. I was one breath away from telling Drew to plow her over. We could swear we thought she was a zombie. This would probably be one of those things that Gordon wanted to keep me from doing to embarrass the Department.

She sidled around the driver's door and Drew powered down the window. The motors in the door sounded strained and stressed. I did not want to talk to this psycho. I was glad she went to the driver's side.

"Can we help you?" Drew asked.

I expected her to lunge in and tear his face off with her teeth, Florida bath salts style. It would be a story we could tell over drinks for years.

She held onto his doorframe hard enough that I heard the inside paneling crackle. If he drove away now, we would drag her. Her fingernails were jagged and caked black underneath with filth that did not look exactly like grease or dirt.

She said, "Don't take those kids."

Drew looked at me and I said, "We're not taking anyone's kids, ma'am. You need to get out of the street."

"That woman is bad. She's a family wrecker and she can't take the girls away from their home. No right person would do that."

"Who, ma'am? Who are you talking about?" I asked. I wanted to ask if this was Ruthie Tanner or someone connected to her. If this drugged out soaking wet bitch was related to her or friends with her, she might end up leading us to her. Sometimes they walked right up. Sometimes they talked about themselves in third person. Occasionally, they told on themselves and made the decisions easier. I didn't want to put the woman's name in this crazy broad's mouth if it wasn't already there. Stirring the psycho pot was not my job.

"They are not her kids." The woman's voice was giving out and turned into gravel in her throat. "They are all our kids."

Drew cleared his throat. "It takes a village."

"Drew." I put my hand on his arm. This one was bordering on threat. I didn't know for sure who she was talking about, but she was moving deeper into trouble. "Whose kids are you talking about? Tell me who you are talking about?"

"You'll find out." Her eyes lost their focus and drifted off center in her head. She let go of the door and strolled back down the driver's side, along the center dotted line of the road. Drew leaned down to watch her in the side mirror.

My phone buzzed in the floorboard and I leaned down to retrieve it. Gordon again. I had three messages from him. I tapped the green answer icon on the screen. "Hey, we were checking on a client. I haven't checked your messages yet."

"Get to the Drake Street house. We have a big problem," Gordon said.

The temporary house. The Walter kids were there. Who else? The father came back for them. He got out of custody and somehow found out where they were. That had to be it.

"What happened, Gordon?"

"I can't describe it. Just get here. Find me before you do anything else. Don't talk to anyone."

He hung up and I lowered the phone. "Oh, shit."

"What is it?" Drew asked.

I turned around and looked over the seat. The

soaking wet bitch was gone. "Where did she go?"

Drew slunk down to look in the mirror again. "She was veering to the left. She might have gone into the ditch. You want to pull back and look for her?"

"No." I scrolled through my coded contacts. "I have a new address for you to put in your phone."

We drove back roads through the suburbs of Atlanta outside the Perimeter. If I had known which way he was going to take us, I would have directed him to take the expressways. I'm not sure that it would have been faster, but it would have felt good to be moving with more speed.

We pulled up along the street. The houses were on one side and a forest of tall, thin pines marked the other side of the road. Piles of limbs covered the ground dead and brown from the last ice storm a couple years ago. I saw the blue lights flashing off the boxy houses to our right before I saw the house we were looking for.

I reached down and silenced the maps app on Drew's phone myself. "Pull up here on the curb and stay in the car until I get back."

"Are you sure, Linda?"

I saw Gordon with his hands on his hips at the edge of the lawn ahead of us. He wore a sports jacket that matched the paint job on the car. He had a pencil thin mustache that would have fit in better in the fifties than it did today. It was the kind of look I associated with guys we would investigate rather than have running the Child Services Department. He stared off into the woods.

"Yeah, I'm sure."

I opened my door before he was at a complete stop. If Drew had kept rolling, we would have taken out a mailbox and a power box on the corner of the lot. I walked toward Gordon without closing the door.

Gordon glanced over at me and then back to the woods. I saw the moisture in his eyes in the flashing lights and I was afraid.

"What happened, Gordon?"

"They are all dead. All of them, Linda. You should thank God you were not here when they took the bodies out."

"Jesus." I looked at the open door of the house, officers going in and out. I had brought the kids here myself not a week ago. I dropped them off before I went to have my arm checked. "Was it the father?"

I thought I already knew the answer.

"He's still in jail," Gordon said. "It was the house parents. The man went ape shit on the wife. The neighbors heard him yelling about women in the walls. They heard him from inside their houses and they called the cops. He killed all three Walters kids, the wife, and himself before the police got here."

"A gun?" I wasn't sure why it mattered, but it was the only words I could make come out. This was a normal house. These were reliable people. That's why we used them for emergency placements. We had used them dozens of times. I had checked the house before I left. Hadn't I? Had I just assumed everything was fine? I wouldn't have seen women in the walls inside the man's head from a visual check. I wouldn't have found a gun, if they hid it either. We checked for padlocks on doors or scratch marks on walls. These were the only levels of crazy we could spot check for.

I wasn't sure if I had gone inside at all now. My arm had been killing me.

"He used a knife," Gordon said. "He stabbed them so many times. He stabbed himself at least a dozen times and sliced himself on both sides of his neck. They'll have to count during the autopsies."

Gordon bowed his head and swallowed several times staring down at the grass.

"Jesus Christ."

He cleared his throat and said, "Every case gets reviewed now. All of them from everyone. Any time we are thinking about moving a child's placement, I need to come out for an additional visit before that call is made. This is going to change things for a while."

"Kids can die being left where they are too, Gordon."

"Don't fuck with me right now, Linda."

"Why did you make me come out here?" I started moving toward the house.

"I didn't know everything that had happened yet. I just got here my … wait. What are you doing? That's a crime scene."

He reached out and grabbed me by my bad arm. I cried out in pain and he let go. Looking back, I'm almost sure he let go for fear of a lawsuit rather than any concern that he might be hurting me.

I made it almost to the door when a person in plain clothes with plastic covers over his shoes stepped out carrying bloody clothes in clear bags. They belonged to one of the girls – the dead Walters girl – the older dead one. The investigator backed up when he saw me coming. Pale light flashed inside from the pictures they were taking. A uniformed officer stepped out and held up his hands to stop me.

I pulled up short and turned away before he had to say anything. I stepped away and sat down on the lawn, facing the woods; Gordon staring at me. My arm was throbbing like the night I dropped those kids off to die.

All I could think about were the Turner girls I had yet to meet and the strange, wet bitch that warned me not to move them – whether she knew she was talking about them or not.

"They're all our kids," I whispered.

Chapter 6
Ruthie Turner

I WAS IN no condition to talk to that woman right now. I had such a sense of dread I thought if I opened the door, the hot wind would rush in and strangle me where I stood. I wondered why my thoughts were so dark and dramatic lately.

The neighbors kept vigil every time a strange car came into the trailer park. I remembered watching a movie about bad cops and gangs once with Foster, where the police car pulled through a neighborhood and everyone called out ahead so there were no surprises.

I'd heard the radio and knew something was wrong in the trailer park right away, and knew it had to do with me.

That was our signal: blasting a radio for a few seconds until the next person down the road picked it up and did the same.

Our signal. Suddenly, after a few weeks, I was as much a resident as anyone else. My mom would've loved to have seen her trailer park trash daughter actually living the dream.

Was the woman coming back to gloat over the

fact she'd taken Heather from me? Stolen my daughter and placed her back with Foster because of my living conditions. Her actions might have cost me my daughters and I didn't want to play nice right now.

I'd spent last night trying to get my head straight, but it wasn't working. I felt like I'd gone on a binge and was coming down off a massive high, even though I'd been good and hadn't gotten out of the car. Or had I? Were the drugs running through my veins right now? Had I gotten so much in me I didn't even remember?

I remembered a young frail Londoner named Sam or Sarah or something with an S in the beginning of her name who'd been in the crack house with me for three days once. She called heroin *gear*, which I thought was funny for some reason. I guess I was high and then everything sounded funny to me, when I was conscious.

It felt like I was coming down from some bad gear right now. I couldn't focus. If I'd opened the trailer door, the woman would've taken me in. Was she the social worker or a cop? I didn't know and it didn't matter. She wasn't going to be on my side.

Shit. Was I scheduled for a visit and I missed it? Would it go against me in court at the next hearing? I scrambled on my couch for the paperwork. I'd need to call in and act like I just missed her.

And then she'll turn around, come back, and arrest me.

Either way I was screwed. I needed to clear my head. I walked to the door, but hesitated. What if she had driven up the road and was still in the trailer park, messing with another mother? Or she was watching to see if I was really home. Would I get in trouble for not answering the door? Would it go in my permanent record?

The trailer smelled like sweat. The air conditioning unit didn't work and when I wiped my brow it felt like enough water sloshed off to fill a kiddie pool.

I looked at the dirty floor, wondering where all the dirt and debris had come from. I always kept a neat and tidy home, even Foster's house. This wasn't my home.

There was a knock on the roof and I jumped, landing awkwardly on an empty box of Ramen and falling to the floor. I was sure it was an acorn falling from the tree above and nothing more, but every sound got under my skin.

Junk mail littered the coffee table and spilled over onto the floor near my face. I wasn't a total cliché yet with a stack of unpaid utility bills, but it wouldn't be long now.

Foster wasn't going to give me a dime until the court ordered it. He made more than enough to give me money for a nicer place to live and child support for the girls. This hell hole was just a temporary stop, something someday I'd look back and laugh at. It wasn't the worst place I'd ever lived, either. In fact, I felt more at home with these trailer park mutants than anyone associated with Foster and his world. It scared me how quickly I could slip back into this part of my former life.

There was another knock at the door. It was the secret knock Xandra from across the street used.

When I opened the door a crack after a struggle to get up and smooth out some of the creases on my blouse, the sunlight smacked me in the face and made me squint.

"Girl, you alright?" Xandra asked. She was already trying to look around me to see if I had a man and/or drugs in the trailer.

"I'm fine," I said and kept a foot behind the door so I could close it if need be. Xandra was nice enough to kill time with, but she was a meth head and drank too much, whining about how the state had unjustly taken her kids. I could definitely see the state's point, but wasn't going to argue. I would always nod my head at the right places and kill some more time with this insane woman.

I think what drew me to Xandra was the fact she was in a position I would've been if Foster hadn't found me. I'd be permanently in this trailer park, looking for the next score and searching for sympathy for my plight.

"I'll be right out," I said and closed the door before she could barge her way inside. I had no delusion she was anything but a druggie and a thief, and didn't want her checking out my meager possessions. I'd done the smart thing and let her come right inside the first time she came over to introduce herself and me to the trailer park. Her eyes had gone over every square inch of the small trailer, looking for valuables and anything to pawn. Xandra was out of luck. I didn't even bother taking a television with me. I had a stack of mystery novels near the couch-bed I knew she wasn't interested in.

I wore the only jewelry I'd taken when I'd left,

and it wasn't much. I kept my credit cards in my pant pocket at all times, even though Foster had blocked me from the accounts. I guess he hoped it would pull me back to the house quicker. I wasn't going to budge if I could help it.

I had about five hundred in cash left to my name, in an envelope taped to the underside of the heavy coffee table. My paychecks went to rent, utilities and gas and didn't leave much else.

I fit right in with these people.

Xandra was waiting for me on the small deck with a cigarette dangling from her mouth and a coffee cup I knew was filled with vodka. She'd start on the Jack and Coke by late afternoon. She said it took the edge off and I couldn't argue. I'd done it myself plenty of times.

You get into the routine of addiction: finding like-minded people who look worse than you think you are and listening to their sorry stories and thanking God you're not half as bad as this loser and that broken person. Even when you do as much meth or heroin as they do, you can justify it because it isn't like you do this much on a daily basis. Of course, as their intake increases, so does yours. As long as you do less than the next person, you're golden.

A normal day becomes sleeping because the light bothers you and the itching isn't so bad when you can't see your bleeding arms or see your blank eyes in a mirror. Lights stay out and shades stay drawn.

I'd once spent nearly a month in a dark bathroom eating peanuts and drinking from a cracked sink. People came and went. I think I slept in the tub, but it's still hazy. I remember someone tying off my arm a few times and pumping drugs into my body so I'd be more pliable. When I came down off a high, I was a fighter.

"You want a sip?" Xandra asked with no intention of sharing her vodka.

"I'm good." I really wanted a cigarette, but I knew better than to bum one off of her. Out here, in the jungle, a minor borrow would be twisted so far I'd be indebted to her to help bury a body. Once I got my shit together today, I'd walk down to the convenience store and count out my pennies.

My cell phone rang in my pocket and I pulled it out, expecting the worst. Before answering, I looked around at the trailers, expecting the social worker to be staring at me, phone to her ear, waiting for me to lie. I should've stayed inside and fought my demons.

It was Maggie.

I covered my mouth when it rang again. Had I missed picking her up? Had I made plans with her and now my oldest was going to question what I was doing and why? She'd know I was sitting on the deck, wasting my day, with one of the horrible trailer park trash women I swore to both my daughters I wouldn't get friendly with.

"You want me to answer it?" Xandra asked, a broad smile on her pale face. She held out her free hand. "If it's your ex-husband, I'll tell him you're busy going down on me. That'll get his sorry ass going."

"It's my daughter," I said as it rang again. "I need to take this."

Xandra shrugged and took a sip. She wasn't going anywhere. She wanted to hear all the juicy gossip.

"Can you excuse me? I'll talk to you later," I said and stood. The phone rang again. If Maggie didn't get an answer, would she be irate? I'd be giving her even more reasons to hate me.

Maggie had stayed with Foster and refused to run away with me, even though she had to know the house was unsafe. Her father was losing his mind and I suppose I was, too.

Xandra threw herself around like a child, but finally got up and off my deck, taking her sweet time going home and trying to listen to my conversation. I wasn't going to give her the satisfaction. I went back inside, the heat and stench stifling. I needed to open all the windows.

"Hello?" I asked on the sixth ring, fearing she'd already hung up.

"Are you busy?" Maggie asked. I could hear the tinge of annoyance and anger in her words. Judging me. She may as well have asked if I had a syringe tied off and a needle in my arm. I was sure Foster had already poisoned the girls about my checkered past and made himself out to look like the big hero.

"No. I was… in the bathroom," I said, images of my month-long stint in a bathroom filling my head. "What's up, honey?"

Maggie paused before answering and I could picture her pursing her lips and rolling her eyes on the other end. My daughters took after me when it came to sarcasm and being annoyed at the slightest things. Three control freak women in the house. Foster never had a chance.

"I want to see you," Maggie finally said.

"Right now?" I asked, hoping there wasn't panic

in my voice. I went to the bathroom and turned on the harsh light. I looked like hell.

"Soon. I need to talk to you. Can you promise to make time for me?"

There it was. The judgment. The kick in the teeth, nice and subtle as usual.

"I'm working tonight. Got some overtime," I lied. "I don't have to go in until noon tomorrow. We can meet for breakfast," I said.

"I have school," Maggie answered quickly, as if she'd been given my answers ahead of time and had practiced the condescending retort.

I was about to ask if Tuesday was better, but I had no idea right then what day it was. "How about the day after?"

"Fine. I guess I'll wait. Can you pick me up at the house?" Maggie asked.

"I was hoping after school." I didn't want to go anywhere near the house or Foster if I could help it.

"I'll call you tomorrow. Hopefully you'll answer the phone," Maggie said with such venom I felt like I'd been smacked.

She knew about all the horrible thoughts in my head and my slow slide into addiction again…

No. I hadn't done anything wrong. I was still clean and sober. I was feeling sorry for myself, but I hadn't fallen off the wagon. Maggie was wrong.

"Hello?" I asked, the phone still pressed against my ear.

Maggie had hung up on me and I was too lost in my own morbid thoughts to hear it.

Chapter 7
Heather Turner

I SHOULD HAVE stayed with mom. I didn't like the apartment or the trailer. I didn't like driving away scared. I didn't like coming back to Atlanta after mom got the phone call. If I knew they were going to take me from her, I would have had to choose whether to fight and run or to give up. Not that it mattered much, but I didn't get the chance to pick a side. I had to watch mom cry as the officer and that Melinda woman took me back to the rainy parking lot to meet dad. If the cop hadn't been there, I wonder if dad would have yelled at me. Instead, I cried and he cried. I wanted to throw up, but I just cried.

Maybe I should have stayed home. If I had refused to go like Maggie had, maybe mom would have stayed too. Maybe we wouldn't be trying to get her back to quiet the things upstairs. Dad still thought Maggie was at school when mom took me. He didn't know that she decided to stay with him. She didn't want him to know for some reason. If I hadn't gone with mom, then none of us would have chosen her and I'm not sure I could live with that.

Maggie hung up the phone and I blinked myself

back into the moment in her room on the bed. I said, "Um, what … Is she coming?"

"Don't know. You know what it's like to get mom to make a decision," Maggie said before rubbing her eyes. It was with the heels of her hands like when an old person is tired and not like when someone is trying clear tears. This house was going to make us all old. No one was allowed to leave.

"When she decided to go, she really went," I said.

"If she was smart," Maggie said as she dropped her hands away from her face, "she wouldn't have turned the car around once child services called. She wouldn't have kept the same cell phone in the first place. They have burners in gas stations for people who don't want to be found."

"Is that how you would have done it, if you had come with us?" As soon as I said it, I was scared. Maggie was too strong and too smart for me. I did not want to be on her bad side.

Maggie said, "If I decided to leave, no one would find me. Not even the ones upstairs."

I swallowed and said, "I believe you."

"Aren't you supposed to be watching for dad?"

The front door opened and both our eyes went wide. We snuck out of her room and down the hall into the living room to find the front door hanging open. Was he bringing in groceries? I thought he was already home.

We walked to the front door and I stayed behind Maggie as we looked out. It occurred to me then that putting Maggie between me and the front door put no one between me and the stairs. I felt cold inside.

Dad was walking down the street. He was

barefoot and carrying a knife. It was a small paring knife, but it was still wrong watching him stroll down the street like that with his face locked forward and his eyes unfocused. Why did none of the neighbors call? Why wasn't Child Services concerned about this? Mom didn't tell on him. She ran away and took me with her because of all of this, but when she had the chance to tell, she didn't. Maybe she thought destroying him would be destroying all of us. Maybe a man that blacked out and took knives out into the neighborhood was the kind of guy that needed destroying – or at least some help.

Maggie pushed the door closed and locked it. "I guess we're on our own for dinner again."

"Should we call someone?" I asked.

"And say what?"

"Exactly what's happening."

"Just the part about dad walking out?" Maggie asked. "Or all of it? The people upstairs? What we saw mom doing before she left?"

I turned and looked up the stairs. I remembered her tying the knots. She was doing it with string, electrical cords, and even her hair. The knots started to look like nooses. She stopped tying them after we left the house.

"Maybe we shouldn't bring her back," I said. "Maybe we should go to her ... both of us. You can help us get burner phones and not get found. Coming back here may have been a mistake, right?"

Maggie stepped around so that she was between me and the stairs. "Don't talk about that kind of stuff in here. I'm doing my best to get everything settled again."

"Why do you stay if you can hear them and see them? I'm afraid to stay here just knowing they're here."

Maggie whispered back. "Leaving doesn't mean anything if the stuff you're running away from can follow you. I'm trying to be part of the solution. That's what we're supposed to do, right? Otherwise, we are just another problem."

I looked up the stairs past Maggie's head and said, "I don't know. I'm scared."

"Stay here. I need to go up to take care of some stuff."

I grabbed Maggie's shoulders. "Don't leave me down here. Dad is gone. Mom is gone. I don't want to be by myself."

"I'll be right back. I have to take care of this thing."

I shook my head. "I'm going with you. Don't leave me down here."

"You don't want to go up there, Heather."

"Don't leave me down here, Maggie. Please."

Maggie sighed and looked over her shoulder. I couldn't tell if she was seeing anything or not. She finally said, "Fine. But do not say anything at all. Not a word once we are up there."

I nodded. "Okay."

As we climbed the stairs, we held hands the way we used to when we were little, back when Maggie first started seeing things before mom and dad did. Or before we knew they did.

We reached the top of the stairs on the second floor, across from the dead animal room. Dad had put up scaffolding and plastic like he planned to paint or redo the wallpaper, but he hadn't done anything and hadn't bought any paint. Maybe that's where he was walking barefoot to when he left out the front door with the paring knife. I wanted to ask Maggie what she was doing, but I kept my mouth closed like I had promised. I had to keep a few of my promises or this place was going to drive me crazy. This whole family was going to drive me crazy including the ones upstairs that I couldn't see.

Maggie spoke all of a sudden and I jumped. She squeezed my hand tighter as she spoke. "I'm not going to the third floor. I have my sister with me." There was a pause. "Why don't you come down here? I've already come halfway and I know you can because I've seen you go outside." She cleared her throat and said, "Fine. I'll come to the foot of the stairs, but don't do anything stupid. I'm not afraid to make trouble for you and you know I will."

Maggie pulled us forward. I was shaking as we walked along the railing and stopped at the foot of the stairs leading up to the third floor. It looked like the side of a mountain to me. She was already staring up. Maggie whispered to me. "Sit down here at the bottom and don't say anything. Not on the step. On the floor. Face away from the stairs."

I sat down like she said, but didn't want to let go of her hand. She had to pry my fingers off of hers. My back was to the mountain of steps leading up to fear.

Maggie said, "I called her. She said she will come tomorrow or the day after."

I looked up at her. Her face looked defiant instead of scared. How did she do that? Not looking scared. I didn't know how to do that. I was scared all the time

—

68

even by the normal stuff in life. How does a person go through life not being scared? I couldn't imagine.

Maggie spoke again to whoever she could see and hear, but I couldn't. Still, she told me to face away from the stairs. Why did she want me to face away? I was afraid to ask because I was afraid she'd tell me the answer. Maggie said, "You need to stop sending him away. If he gets caught out there, they'll take all of us away and there'll be nothing you can do about it. They'll probably tear the house down and build a coffee shop."

I listened to the house creak and pop, expecting angry cracks to split through the floor and ceiling. I heard nothing else.

Maggie said, "It's your own fault then. If we're working for the same thing, you need to act like we're on the same side."

I shook my head. Who was she making deals with?

"Then, you convince them to behave. I can't do everything. They're your problem. That is third floor business. Your business."

How many things were in this house? Maggie shifted her feet. She was standing with them planted farther apart like she expected to get hit and was bracing herself.

"You leave her out of this or we're through."

A lump caught in my throat. Were they talking about my mother or me?

"Fine. But I'm only fourteen. There is only so much I can do." She sighed and added. "It doesn't matter what they did when they were fourteen because they can't do it now, can they?" She sniffed and said, "Well, that doesn't appear to be helping, does it?" Maggie gave a few grunts over a long stretch like she was listening to instructions. "Tell me. Were you alive back when you took care of dad after they died?"

I felt dizzy. If I wasn't already sitting on the floor, my feet would have gone out from under me. Talking to ghost about dying in the place they controlled felt like a big mistake. It felt like grabbing a snake by the tail.

Maggie said, "Are they here now?" Then she added "Do you get stuck here if you die or if you get murdered here?"

I whispered, "I want to go."

"Shut up," Maggie hissed back. She took a step forward, putting herself between me and the third floor stairs. I couldn't see her feet anymore, but I was afraid to turn around. I had already broken one promise. Maggie said, "What happens to spirits that don't end up stuck here in the house? Where do they go?" She waited a moment and then said, "Maybe I just want to know." Then, she added. "Ask a priest? Really? That's hilarious coming from you. Why don't you actually go to Hell then?" Another pause where I waited for cracks to form and the house to explode in rage. The silence was almost scarier. "If you care about any of us, you'll stop all of that anyway. If you don't really care about us, then you need to let us go."

Maggie reached down and took my hand again. She pulled me to me feet, but I was still afraid to turn around to face the stairs. She said, "Well, that's your decision, but you better make it quick because this family is falling apart because of you. Come on,

Heather, we're going."

As we walked back along the railing, I asked, "Going? Leaving the house?"

"Just going back downstairs."

I felt my heart sink.

Chapter 8
Ruthie Turner

I WENT TO sleep with my arms itching, never a good sign. It meant I needed a fix even though I was clean. I needed to stay away from bad neighborhoods and bad thoughts right now.

Xandra had knocked on the door after dinner time, but I kept quiet and she eventually gave up and went away. I knew she was watching my front door to see if I was hiding. I'd felt trapped inside even though I had no intention of going out.

I needed to straighten up the trailer in case the girls came over anytime soon. Did Heather or Maggie live with me anymore? I couldn't form coherent thoughts.

The trailer never got cleaned up. The dishes still sat piled in the sink and I didn't have a vacuum cleaner. Or did I? Was it tucked away in the hall closet? In the end, I'd sat down on the old couch and cried and stared at the dark dried spot on the ceiling where the rain got in. Water washed away everything eventually.

I wondered what else could get into the trailer.

Leaving the house hadn't stopped some of the bad

things from happening. The things I couldn't see but knew were there still plagued me. I was being watched at all times. I was being tested to find the rest of my weaknesses.

I was losing my mind.

Sleep came easily, which was a rare gift these days. I had work in the morning. I think I did anyway. I dreamed of nothing, as far as I could tell, because when I woke, not to the sickly yellowed weak rays of the sun but to darkness and heat, I couldn't remember nightmares or pretty fleeting thoughts.

I wasn't ever much of a dreamer that I could remember, even as a child. Sleep wasn't an escape for me, only meant to re-energize my body but not the mind. I was too practical. There was nothing in your dreams that was real or could affect you. I remember someone telling me as a child if you dreamed you died, you died in real life. It wasn't true or I'd be dead a few times from what I could remember.

I coughed, bringing me out of my inane thoughts.

I was going to die in the real world if I didn't get up and get out.

There was an overabundance of smoke in the trailer and at first I thought I'd fallen asleep without turning off a burner and something had burned in a rusting pot. There was too much smoke, though, and the spot on the ceiling where the rainwater liked to sneak inside was gone. Replaced with an angry orange lick of flame dancing in all directions.

The trailer was on fire and I would die from smoke inhalation or my skin fried to a crisp.

There were two smoke detectors in the trailer, but I had no idea if they'd gone off before being engulfed in flames or if they even had batteries in them.

I rolled onto the floor and tried to crawl, through the billowing smoke, to the door but now I had no idea where the door was. Something creaked overhead, but I didn't look up because of all the small debris starting to fall on and around me.

If this was the way I was to die, it would suit me fine, I thought sourly. Reduced to a statistical death as a low income trailer park trash former drug addict separated from her husband and family. I'd be a five minute blip on the local news, where the wide shots of the trailer burning to the foundation would be more important than my name.

I wasn't moving, too wrapped up in my last pity party.

My arms still itched so I knew I was alive, but didn't know for how long. God, why was I such a mess?

The papers and garbage I'd tossed onto the tattered rug, with thoughts of someday picking up, became a field of smaller fires in my path. The rug, coated with body oil and hair and years of unknown fluids and substances, was a series of five foot pillars of flame in spots. The fire was greedily sucking all of the moisture it could like the carpet was bathed in gasoline.

I felt heat on my head and slapped my hair, fearful it had sparked. When was the last time I'd really washed my hair? The clothes I'd fallen asleep in hadn't been washed and I'd worn them a few times. More oils and filth to hug the flames.

I heard sirens now in the distance. I wondered if they were too far to reach me in time. I got onto my knees and scuttled forward, feeling silly, as if someone would take a video of how funny I looked and send it to a funny video show.

As if I mattered enough to get onto TV, even for something as dramatic as dying in a fire.

Heather and Maggie came to mind and the idea of never seeing them again swept through me. What twisted story would Foster give them about my death? Would I someday be replaced by another woman who the girls would call mom? I knew it didn't make any sense, but it spurred me to crawl faster, swiping the burning junk out of my path.

I made a beeline to the door with smoke like cement pressing down on my frail body, trying to drive me into the dirty carpet and pin me so the fire could catch me.

Do it for the girls. Do it so Foster doesn't win.

The door was locked as I slammed my fist against it. Did I have the strength to open it? I knew I didn't. I could barely keep my head off the rug, yet I was expected to reach up several feet and disengage the lock and swing open the door. It was never going to happen.

I crawled as close to the door as I could manage, coiling as tight as possible and feeling the heat at my back. My head pressed against the fake wood and hands covering my mouth and nose, I prayed to a God I didn't know if I still believed in to save me. Open the door and let me live another day. I didn't want to lose my children and have Foster and the house win. I needed to survive and fight another day.

My eyes were watering so badly I closed them, the coolness of my tears rolling down my cheeks and giving my warm skin a reprieve. I pictured the tears never making it to the carpet, becoming steam and mixing with the death all around me.

The noise was suddenly unbearable, cracking timber and popping objects from the kitchen, glasses shattering and the walls buckling under the pressure. I wondered if I'd die from smoke, fire or the trailer collapsing on top of me, or a combination of the three.

I wondered if my daughters would be able to survive in the Turner house and if they'd break like I did. Would Foster protect them? I doubted it. He might only be holding back because I was still in the picture. If I was gone…

I felt the tears, now as hot as the flames surrounding me, streaming from my eyes. I tried to keep them shut, but they hurt. Everything hurt. I prayed I'd pass out soon and wouldn't feel the fire charring my flesh and cooking my organs.

I felt my arm yanked like I was being attacked. I remembered the time, living on the streets of the Combat Zone in Boston for one winter, when I'd been dragged from my makeshift tent and beaten by a psychotic woman who swore I was The Antichrist. The attack brought me a broken arm and nose as well as fourteen stitches, and the desire to never spend another minute in Boston.

I'd forgotten about the Boston trip, like so many others I'd taken because I followed the trail of drugs and bad decisions.

"Ma'am, can you hear me?"

I opened my bloodshot eyes, filled with tears and soot, and blinked until I could make out vague shapes. The first thing I noticed was cool fresh air getting sucked into my mouth and I drank it greedily.

I coughed once, then twice, then I couldn't stop.

There were many people surrounding me when I finally stopped coughing and wiped the spit and grime from my mouth and the tears from my eyes.

I was somehow outside, sitting on the bumper of an ambulance, while the trailer park burned around us.

An EMT and two firefighters were crowding me, and when I put up my hands they stepped back so I could taste more air.

I tried to stand, but my legs wouldn't work properly. I was so weak. I let the EMT move me to a gurney, where I crawled on top by myself and coughed for awhile.

"You stupid bitch, what did you do?" It was Xandra, wearing nothing but an ill-fitting red bra and light blue thong, running at me. I had the absurd thought to laugh at her for not matching her undergarments.

A police officer intercepted Xandra, trying to keep his hands away from her delicate parts, although you'd be hard-pressed to find them on her worn body. Her arms moved in time with her fake boobs and I think I managed a smile, because she was even more furious.

"She set the fire herself. She's crazy," Xandra yelled, trying to get away from the police officer. "I'm going to punch her lights out. Everything I worked so hard for is gone thanks to her."

It was true. Her trailer was ablaze, both rows of trailers on either side glowing like a Christmas display. It was cold out, but the heat from the fire was keeping me warm.

"How do you know it was her?" the cop was asking, trying unsuccessfully to calm Xandra.

"It had to be her. She acts strange. She's a newcomer. She thinks she's better than us," Xandra was saying. She stopped struggling. "Check her trailer for heroin. She's a junkie and an addict."

That wasn't true. Technically, I was clean. It was her word against mine, and I'd done nothing wrong.

The cop was looking at me and now another one was walking over. I'd dealt with enough cops in my life to know I was guilty before I'd said a word. I was either going to jail tonight or to the hospital.

I began to cough again and let it go until I closed my eyes and let the coughing fit take over and knock me out.

I woke hours later in a hospital bed with a police officer standing in the doorway. He whistled for a doctor when he saw my eyes open.

"You didn't test positive for heroin or any illegal substance," the doctor said without so much as a hello or introduction. He stopped at the foot of the bed and frowned. "You're a very lucky woman."

"Because I'm not on drugs?" I asked.

His frown deepened. "You're lucky because you suffered no burns on your body despite being within inches of the fire. Your lungs seem fine and your vitals are strong. You passed out for a few hours and we gave you some meds to keep you stable until we were sure you didn't have internal injuries."

"I appreciate the concern. Can I go?" Even the talk of drugs made me want to lick my lips in anticipation like the old days, even though I'd sworn to never use again.

"You can go once you answer a few questions from the police. Do you have anywhere to go?" the doctor asked.

I did, but it wasn't somewhere I wanted to go. I simply nodded and started to cry.

The doctor's face softened. "I'm really sorry."

I didn't know what he was sorry for or why I was being treated like a criminal. I'd done nothing wrong. Had I?

I sat up in the bed and absently swiped at my hair while three more officers entered the room, crowding around my bed. Air cushions in the bed inflated and deflated with my new position to try to support my weight more comfortably. Fancy. It felt like I was sitting on something alive.

"Have I done something wrong?" I asked.

"Tell me everything you remember," one of the cops said.

I told them what little I did remember: waking to the heat and smoke, crawling to the door and being outside for some reason.

"Firefighters kicked in the door right before the roof collapsed. They heard you tapping against it. You're very lucky. Several people have died. The trailer park is totaled. A couple of your neighbors have pointed a finger at you, accusing you of setting the blaze."

"I didn't do it," I said, wondering if I sounded guilty. I was innocent.

"The fire started outside your trailer. We can tell that already," one of the police officers said. He was trying to act casual, but I could see the look in his eyes. Like every other cop I'd run into in the past. I was about to get harassed or arrested or worse.

"Is there someone we can call to pick you up? We'd like to talk with you tomorrow afternoon," another cop said. He was also looking at me oddly.

Who could they call? My daughters weren't old enough to drive or pick me up. I had no friends to speak of. If I called my employer, I might get fired. I had to go to work… when? I didn't even know what time it was. Everything I owned was now gone. My clothes. My hidden cash. All of it.

The only person I could think of was Foster.

Chapter 9
Foster Turner

I CAME BACK to myself staring down into the trunk of the car at some bag of skin and bones wearing a red bra and a blue thong. Her hair was thin and dark. It was tied up on top of her head with a rubber band. For a moment I thought she was dead and then I became aware that I was holding a steak knife. It was one from the set at our house – the house. I thought I had gotten rid of them all. I turned the blade over slowly in my grip looking for a bloodstain. It would be like I had cut into an extra rare steak – one with mismatched bra and thong. The blade was clean and she, whoever she was, took a deep breath. I could see every one of her ribs imprinted through her skin on the exhales.

My eyes burned and I smelled acrid stench in my nose. It was the smell of shit burning that had no business burning. We once had fires in sheds where fuel tanks blew up a few years back. It was a total property loss. It was burned rubber and cans of paint that boiled and burst. The insulation was wet from the fire fighters and still smoldered. The carpet rolls and repossessed plastic items from one of the properties had been in there. It was what I imagined Hell smelling like if I ever ended up there and it is what I smelled right then, staring down at some stranger in her underwear in a trunk.

I took a step back from the trunk and the body of the scrawny woman I was standing over with my steak knife. I saw white smoke wafting up past the trees. There were clear lights strobing up into the leaves from whatever scene was past the trees.

I was barefoot. Of course, I was. Why wouldn't I be barefoot while committing a murder in Hell? The Cadillac was an older model and rusted out on the sides. I didn't recognize it, the woman, or where I was.

I heard the passenger's side door of the car grind on the hinges and bang closed. So, how was I going to explain this?

I stared at him, leaning on the side of the car, near the open trunk. He was wearing a linen shirt with soft stripes and the sleeves rolled up to just below his elbows. He had on baggy khakis that billowed out from his legs in a way that reminded me of a samurai. He had on his lime green boat shoes. I had never seen that color shoe on any other human being. He had on a felt hat with the flaps tied up on the sides and he wore sunglasses that bled color from the top of the lenses to the bottom running from light brown to pinkish-red.

I cleared my throat and held out the knife to him. "What the hell, Uncle Duke?"

He shrugged, "What the hell, indeed? You picked a heck of a time to wake up, kid."

"What did you make me do this time, Duke?"

"It's like being hypnotized, kid. I can't make you do anything that you don't want to do deep down somewhere."

I looked at the unconscious woman in the trunk and licked my lips. "Did I do this to her?"

Duke tilted his head and curled up his lip on one side. "She smoked up and passed out in her open trunk herself. You closed it and drove her out here before you shook me off and started asking questions."

"I don't want to do any of this," I said.

"You trying to convince me, Foster, or yourself? Because we are on a bit of a tight schedule here. Lots of moving parts if you can get your slutty, blue panties out your crack and get on board with the solution."

"I don't want to put women in trunks for whatever sick plan you have, Uncle Duke," I said. "I sure don't want to wander out of my house in the middle of the night to God knows where."

"That's the thing, Foster. It's like I told you. Some part of you wants to run away or we couldn't get you to do it. Part of you wanted to come out here to collect Ruthie again." Duke nodded toward the smoke.

"This is where she is?" I looked toward the trees again. A voice squawked over a radio that echoed out from the direction of the smoke. "What did you do to her?"

"She made it out alive," Duke said. "Barely made it out, granted, but fully alive."

I turned and took a step toward him holding out the knife. He stared at me, without flinching through his brown and red sunglasses. Why would he be scared? There was nothing I could do to him even though he had done plenty to me.

I whispered, "What if she hadn't?"

"We get her back home either way," Duke said, "but she did make it out, so let's not argue what if's and why not's. If you had just set the fire like I told you, we could have contained it, but you made me use someone outside of the family and now we have to deal with her."

Duke nodded toward the trunk. He waved his open hand over the woman's body with his wrist limp like he was pointing out an unsavory mess on the rug. I looked from her back to my uncle.

"What are you talking about? Who set the fire, Duke?"

Duke sighed and said, "She did, dummy. She was easy enough to use. Like I said, we can't make you do what you don't want and this crazy chicken sure does want to see the world burn. Problem was once she started, she couldn't stop until the whole park was on fire. Reminded me of your daddy in that way. Couldn't stop once he got started either. It was just you and me after that, huh, kid?"

"Go to Hell, Duke."

"Easy, kid." Duke waved both hands at me in one lazy flap. "If I was ever going to Hell like all the tent preachers my momma took me to said I would, I got sidetracked a long time ago. Good thing for you too or you would have had no one to take care of you after the little spat between your folks that day."

"Stop it, Duke."

Duke shrugged. "You're right. Back to business.

This underwear model here came out of it after everything was ablaze and went bonkers. After they took Ruthie away to get checked out at the hospital, I had to convince this one to dose up on the crystals hidden under her seat and then you to drive her out here to finish it."

I tossed the knife down on the ground. "I won't."

Duke licked his teeth and shook his head. "You don't want to leave that there. Fingerprints and it is part of a set, genius. If the chicken here disappears, they are going to figure out that all the fire implements trace back to her and she must have bailed. That's ideal at this point. She's too much of a wildcard to leave loose in the wind. She's got an attachment to Ruthie and might try to track her down, I'm afraid. I know crazy and obsessed when I see it. She saw you before I could put her under my spell."

Duke wiggled his fingers in the air.

"This has to stop, Duke. You've gone too far. Even for you."

Duke shrugged. "All right then. We have to at least get her to a hospital, right? Get in the chariot and drive."

The passenger's door creaked and slammed again and I didn't see Duke anymore. The thing was I realized I had never actually seen the door open. It was a sound effect with no physical explanation. I'd seen and heard similar things from him over the years.

"Bring the knife too." Duke's voice came muffled from inside the car.

I opened the back passenger's door and tossed the knife into the floorboard caked with wet sand and molded fast food cups. I grabbed the woman by her shoulders and dragged her body out of the trunk. Her limbs were hinged sticks that flopped in every direction. Her bare heels dragged the ground, from the trunk, around to the open door.

"What the hell are you doing, kid?" Duke glanced over the seat at me. He no longer had the hat or glasses. His hair looked thin and greasy. I could never understand why his hair changed from visit to visit.

"I'm not driving her around in the trunk." I grunted as I slid her onto the seat. She smelled like piss and something else dirty I couldn't quite place. I closed the door and then closed the trunk.

I considered dragging her back out and leaving her on side of the trail. If she really set the fires like Duke said, they could figure it out without me there. Of course, that left me walking away from my estranged wife's burned trailer park bare foot or stealing a car from the same park.

I opened the driver's door. The noise was different from the one I imagined from Duke's door. I sat down behind the wheel, on the bench seat, next to my uncle. His shoes were light blue now and his sleeves were rolled down, but still unbuttoned. His hair was a little thicker and quaffed up.

The keys dangling from the ignition had a few dozen key chains. I saw an Indian with a bent nose and a full headdress of feathers. Another showed a penguin holding up a mug of frothing beer.

I asked, "Whose car is this?"

Duke cocked a thumb over the seat causing his unbuttoned cuff to flap open and away from his wrist. "The chicken's."

—

86

"Why did you try to burn my wife?"

Duke sighed and closed his eyes. "Wasn't trying to burn her. Needed to burn her out. She has no where to go, so once you drop the chicken off at the coop, you need to be by the phone for Ruthie to call her hero just like always."

Duke opened his eyes and I closed mine. I said, "You're going to kill my family."

"Trying to keep you together ... all of us together."

I started the car and opened my eyes. Something was hammering in the engine before it leveled out to a steady pinging. I opened my eyes. I felt my phone in my pocket and wrestled it out. The battery was missing off the back.

"Where is it?"

Duke snickered and said, "You finish with the chicken and I'll tell you where you put it."

I shook my head. "You had me hide it from myself? Was that something I wanted to do too?"

"You apparently have a deep desire to punish and torture yourself, Foster. Rings true, don't you think?"

"Why don't you deal with cell phone batteries and starting fires yourself?" I asked. "Why do you get other people to do your dirty work for you? I've seen you touch and move things."

"Tough to explain," Duke said, "My current condition didn't come with an instruction manual, but near as I can tell, I mostly can't move stuff I didn't touch in life. I can move stuff in the house when needed. Didn't have any fancy space phones in my day, so I have to use you for that."

"I need to call the girls. Every time you run me

out of the house, you put them in danger."

"The sassy girl said the same thing before I left the house," Duke said.

My throat went dry and I could feel my heart hammering harder than the unconscious meth head arsonist's Cadillac engine. I licked my lips again, but my tongue felt like sandpaper. "I don't want you talking to them. That was the deal."

Duke stared forward through the windshield. He finally said, "People spend their entire lives trying to make deals with the afterlife. Never quite works out though. You'd rather them talk to me than the others, wouldn't you?"

"I don't like any of this."

"Start driving, Foster."

I shifted into drive and followed the dirt trail until we reached a paved road. "Which way?"

"Take a right."

I followed along. We passed the smoking hulks of the trailers. Fire trucks filled the spaces between as people in blankets hugged each other.

"Jesus Christ, Duke."

"Wasn't that nice of a place before, I assure you."

Blue lights flashed from behind. I looked in the rearview mirror at the approaching patrol car. There were two women in the back seat. The meth head was still unconscious, but her head was in the lap of a soaking wet woman in a nightgown.

"Let me do all the talking," Duke said.

"That's not funny."

I pulled off to the side of the road. The police car raced past us. I sat there holding the steering wheel, shaking.

"You just need to trust me, Foster."

"Give me my phone battery or I'm not going anywhere."

Duke sniffed. "You want to stay here until you're caught for real? What happens to the girls then?"

"I'll let Ruthie have the kids and we'll leave the house empty."

Duke glared at me. "Don't joke like that, kid. The others don't find you as clever or charming as I do. When they start making plans, they play for keeps. That's what happened to your parents, remember?"

"The battery."

Duke looked out his window. "Under your seat. Be careful. There may still be some crystals under there or maybe some razor blades or a possum."

I found it and locked it back on my phone. I didn't know where my case was, but that seemed less pressing. I waited as the silver apple sat on the screen as the phone reloaded. I unlocked it with my thumb and it rang. I was sure my girls were scared out of their minds. I had no idea how long I'd been gone.

"Hello?"

There was a pause and I was about to say something else when I heard her say, "Foster?"

"Ruthie? What's … What's going on?"

Duke winked at me. The soaking wet woman was staring at me in the rearview mirror still. I started to remember seeing her from the house. It was after my parents died. Maybe ten years ago? I couldn't remember. She was from the third floor. What was she doing out here?

"Did you set the fire?" Ruthie asked.

I took a deep breath. "I didn't set any fire. Are

you okay?"

It was a rare moment that I could actually get away with the truth.

"I need somewhere to go."

"I don't understand, Ruthie. Do you want to come home?"

"Will you pay for a hotel room until we work things out between us?"

I felt the burn in my throat like I was back in the smoke. "You're unbelievable. If you want to try to take our children and run off, you are on your own with that and any trouble it brings you."

"Do you want to come get me then?"

I swallowed twice. "I … It could take me a while, but I'll get there. I was out taking care of some work stuff. Tell me where you are and I'll call you back once I'm on the way … I can bring the girls too."

I heard a noise I was sure was her stifling tears. She coughed and said, "Will you cover the cab if I take one back to the house? If I decide that instead of you coming to get me once they release me? I'm not saying I'm coming back. I may not even come inside, but we need to talk, I guess."

I swallowed again. I wasn't even sure how far I was from home. I needed to shower. I thought I might smell like smoke and that wouldn't be good. I needed to get rid of the stolen car and the half naked overdose in the back

"Okay. Whatever you … okay. Call me before you get ready to leave the hospital or wherever you are." I heard the phone click from the other end of the connection. Was she on her way now? "Hello? Ruthie?"

I pulled the phone away from my ear. The knife flashed by my face and cracked the screen. My phone flipped out of my hand and then the skinny wrist was coming back across for another slash. I pulled the handle to open the car door and tumbled out onto the westbound lane of the road.

The wet woman in the back was still staring. Duke was wearing his sunglasses again and shaking his head as the woman in her red bra waved around my steak knife.

Duke said, "Should have left her in the trunk, kid."

The woman's dark hair fell loose around her face from her rubber band. She looked around the inside of the car. "Who are you people?"

Chapter 10
Xandra

THE GUY IN the passenger seat was smiling at me, but not leering, even though I was almost naked in the backseat of the car.

I had a faint smell of mold and wetness before I shook my head and tried to figure out how I'd gotten in this predicament. The driver's door was open and I got the sensation of movement.

The car was moving without a driver.

"I'd put your seatbelt on, chicken," the guy said to me a second before we slammed into a tree or another car or something.

THE WOMAN WAS staring at me, looking like she

wanted to cry. Her eyes were ringed black. Could have been from being strung out, but she looked like a drowned rat.

I tried to get up and realized I was duct taped to a chair, still in my bra and thong. My ass felt raw and splintered on the old wooden chair. Now I was pissed.

"Let me go. Untie me," I said, giving the bitch the nastiest stare I could manage. I was still a little high and didn't want to come down just yet. Drug strength was what my first ex-husband used to call it. I'd suck the glass dick and fight three men in a bar and not worry about my broken hand or bruised ribs for two days until I came down.

I smelled mold and the faint trace of wet soap, like someone had stepped out of a shower. Even though the room I was in was bare and dark, I could see the woman was wet from head to toe like she'd showered in her nightgown.

She didn't move when I told her to untie me. She was just staring, occasionally blinking her big, bruised doe eyes and moving her fingers slightly.

"Can you at least tell me where I am?"

I'd be lying if I said I hadn't been in a similar situation a couple of times in my life. I remembered living with Raul in Panama City and a rival gang had busted in and tortured Raul while I had to watch. Some nightmares still had his bloody face in them and I missed the guy too. He'd been a loyal friend, lover, and provider. Stealing from a rival gang wasn't the smartest thing to do. I still didn't know where they'd buried his body parts, even though I'd taken up with the guys that had beaten and killed him in order to save my own ass.

My ass that was rubbing against this horrible chair. I could feel the slight pain as I came down. I looked to see if I was bleeding, but it was too dark. I imagined my ass was a bloody mess, and I could now feel my wrists rubbing against the splintered wood of the chair.

She wasn't going to be helpful. Probably a lackey to whoever had kidnapped me. I remembered being in the trailer and feeling like I wasn't alone. Had there been a fire? I moved my face close to my shoulder and smelled smoke. What had happened?

The door to the room opened a crack and faint light spilled in from a hallway.

"Hello?" I asked. What else did I have to lose?

No answer and the bitch kept staring, standing still except for the eyes blinking and fingers moving at her side. I wondered if she was also high and what she was on, because I needed some.

My eyes adjusted to the empty room, only now I saw it wasn't as empty as I thought it was.

In the left corner, away from the door, three children sat perfectly still. I thought they were life-size dolls until one of them moved an arm. Maybe I could sweet talk them into untying me. Kids were stupid.

"Hey, can you do me a big favor and untie me? I really need to get home. I have candy in my pocket," I said.

"You don't have pockets," one of the kids said. It was a little girl.

All three kids stood and I saw it was two girls and a boy.

The boy was grinning from ear to ear.

I smiled back. "What's your name, sweetie?"

"Clifford. Everyone calls me Cliff. I can see your boobies."

I laughed and stuck them out. He was maybe ten, but his hormones had already kicked in and I wanted to get him over to me to get me out of this before his daddy or whoever else was here came back. I remembered the creepy guy from the car. Was this his family? Was I going to be featured a few years from now in an *Investigation Discovery* episode? I hoped so, but hoped I was alive to tell my side of the story.

"Have you ever touched them in real life?" I asked, feeling a little creepy myself. I was trying to seduce a child, but it was kill or be killed, right?

The door opened with a squeal and the guy from the car was standing there, grinning, with an unlit cigar dangling from his lips. From the light behind him, I could see how oily and slick his hair was.

"I see you've met part of the extended family, chicken," he said slowly, each word spilling out in cadence. He was clearly amused at having me in this predicament.

"I don't know what you've done to me and I don't care. Let me go and I won't tell a soul. I swear. I have warrants for my arrest in Florida and won't go to the cops," I said. The warrant stuff was true, but, if this scumbag let me go, I was going to the nearest police station and crying them a river.

"Oh, you won't go to the cops is right... unless you do as I say," he said. "If you play nice and follow the rules, you'll be allowed to leave. Hell, I'll even make sure you're dropped off at the police station with a pen in hand for your written account of what happened. How does that sound?"

I didn't know if he was lying or not, but I'd been in these situations before and needed to keep my wits and my charm intact. Guys were all the same: they wanted to feel like they had the upper hand. As long as you lied and told them it was more than big enough and you moaned loud, they gave you a pass on the rest of it.

I casually spread my legs as far as I could with the binding and hoped he didn't get I was doing it on purpose. His eyes went to my crotch and I could see the cigar was about to fall out of his mouth.

"Everybody, leave the room," he said, his voice low but powerful.

The room cleared immediately, leaving the two of us alone. This was going to be another turning point in my life.

I thought back to the week I'd worked as a stripper in Jacksonville at that dingy club. On the third night, after the place had closed and the last of the losers had been escorted out, the three bouncers had bought me drink after drink and told me how I was the best stripper they'd ever seen. I'd given a couple of blowjobs to them just for fun and even finished off the DJ in his booth. They told me I was special.

Like an idiot, I believed every word of it.

When I'd woken in the bathroom of the club the next morning, covered in filth and semen, I'd felt humiliated. They'd not only taken turns with me when I passed out, but started scribbling horrible words on my body in permanent marker and covering me with skunked beer and the garbage from the night before.

I worked for three more shifts that week, ignoring their jeers and the customers asking why I had WHORE and SLUT written on my ass and thighs. The cool part is it turned some guys on and I had some huge tips those nights before management finally told me not to come back.

The greasy guy was suddenly hovering over me, blocking the light from the open door.

"Here's how this is going to play out ... you're going to keep your mouth shut so Foster doesn't have to gag you. He's really sloppy with duct tape in case you couldn't tell. If he has to cover your mouth, I'm afraid he'll accidentally get your nose, too. That sounds like a horrible way to die, don't you think?"

I nodded my head. I didn't know who Foster was and hoped this nutcase wasn't talking in third person. That would be crazy.

Then, it hit me. Foster was the asshole husband of Ruthie from the trailer park. What did he have to do with any of this?

"A car is going to pull up any minute and people will be entering the house. If you so much as fart, I will have to end your life. Are we on the same page so far, chicken?"

I nodded again. I had no doubt this guy wasn't much of a bluffer. There were two of them and it connected to Ruthie in some way. "My car?"

He looked confused for a second before taking the cigar out of his mouth and grinning.

"Your car is at the bottom of a retention pond a couple of miles from here. They'll never find it or you. The last anyone saw of sweet half-naked Xandra

---

97

was you screaming and yelling at Ruthie and the cops about wanting to kill her. See, if she comes up dead, they'll have you to blame. We don't want Ruthie dead, though. We need her. You? ... We need you as long as you're useful and follow directions to the letter," he said and put the cigar back in his mouth before turning and heading to the door.

The light returned, pushing away the darkness around me.

"What do you want me to do? I want to help so I can live," I said, trying not to sound too desperate but failing.

He stopped in the doorway, but didn't turn back around.

"I want you to remember how serious all of this is. I need you to know the importance of you being absolutely still and silent when they arrive. If I hear the chair slide across the floor or you calling out or anything, I will have no choice but to torture you and, eventually, have you killed," he said.

"I understand." I wouldn't do anything unless I thought I had a decent chance of escaping from this house. I didn't even know where I was, but hoped I was somewhere close to the police or at least other people who could help me.

"The children will be nearby, but out of sight. Listening for anything stupid from you, chicken. I won't waste my time warning you again," he said and closed the door, leaving me in darkness once more.

I decided to slowly and quietly work on my duct taped hands.

That's when I heard the car.

Chapter 11
Ruthie Turner

I EXPECTED HIM to ask me what had happened or if I was okay. I expected him to try to hold me, but he stood at a distance in front of where they had wheeled me out in the chair and left me. The doctors and the police were done with me for now. Only the house wanted me and maybe still Foster. Maybe …

Foster said, "Is there anything you need to get before we go back … before we go?"

He was afraid that if he told me we were going back to the house, then I would jump up and run away even with my lungs feeling like I'd been punched in the chest a few times. Maybe I just might.

"No, all my stuff was burned," I said.

He stood there looking away. "The car is over here."

I started to stand, but then wavered on my feet a little. He reached out to steady me even though he was standing too far away to make contact. I looked at his hand as I regained my balance and he withdrew his reach.

We stood in silence a moment longer with siren sounds approaching on the other side of the hospital. He turned toward the parking lot and I followed, on his flank, out of his reach. I could smell the smoke on my clothes, even outside, like I had been bathing in the scent. I had no other clothes to change into ... except back at the house.

He opened my door for me. I didn't see him do it, but he was standing there holding the open passenger's door. I bowed my head and stepped into his car, scooting over in the seat. I felt like a criminal being put in the patrol car for the ride to my holding cell. I kind of expected him to put his hand on my head as he guided me in, but he didn't. The authorities had finally apprehended me. Burning me out of the trailer had to be some kind of entrapment.

I had a moment then that I felt like this was a mistake. This felt like my last chance to get away. I wouldn't have my girls, but maybe that was how it had to be. This was me sliding into the trap with the guy I thought had set the fire. He was taking me back to the place of nightmares.

"Watch your ... ugh ..." He pointed down, but couldn't seem to find the word foot in his college level vocabulary.

I pulled my foot into the car and I saw he was wearing sneakers without socks. That wasn't really his thing. I thought about his barefoot adventures during the night. He had small coin-sized bruises on his shins.

Foster closed my door and came around to his side of the car. He pulled out of the space and we were on our way back like my escape had meant nothing. I glanced over at his face. My leaving and his staying had changed everything for all of us.

He said, "Heather got back into school okay. She's catching back up on work."

I mouthed the word okay, but I couldn't get any breath behind it. I wanted to believe it was the smoke, but I think I just couldn't bring myself to declare that everything or anything was okay. Because it wasn't. He didn't see me mouth it out, so it was like I said nothing. The word was a ghost and unlike most of the ghosts in our lives, it went unseen.

"I put up some scaffold and plastic," he said as he made a turn. "Think I'll finally fix up the second floor."

I looked down into my lap and folded my hands. I tried to nod my head, but I'm not sure how it looked with my head at that angle. I felt blood throbbing in the veins in my forehead, but I kept my head bowed.

He was never going to agree to let the house go. This was the deal breaker between both of us and for both of us. This was the end of negotiation. Management and labor were leaving the table. The wife was walking out and the husband was staying. We were both haunted by it all, but we had chosen opposite solutions and we were dug into our positions. These were the most irreconcilable of irreconcilable differences. The final sticking point was our girls. He was going to get the house and everything in it without a fight. He wanted the girls to stay and I wanted them to go. He had the house and the stable job. I was the mother and had a history of drug use. I was back in the car on the way back to the house, so maybe I had already lost this in every way that mattered. I felt like I had lost.

If we could unite again as a team, we might win. We had beaten everything else from drug habits to marital spats. The drive to leave and the drive to stay was the wedge between us. If there was no give on that, then the team was split. For us to unite, one would have to give up all the ground. There was no middle ground left between our positions. In any marriage, the loss of middle ground was the end. This situation with this house was no exception. We each saw the other's position as the death of everything. The other was ruining everything with his or her choice.

Minutes passed with pauses at stop signs and the sound of wheels burning away asphalt, closing the miles back to the place I couldn't seem to leave.

Foster cleared his throat and I startled, but wouldn't look up. He said, "Maggie dyed her hair. It's red. Almost purple. I think she did it to …"

I waited for the end of the sentence. Was he going to blame me or himself for her rebellion? The next word never came. A minute passed along with more road and then another minute. He seemed to be done talking.

I still didn't look up, but I said, "I don't have any answers about any of this, Foster. Things are bad … there. I just couldn't anymore. I couldn't put the girls … I just couldn't. I don't think you're a bad person. That's not why. That house makes it all bad though. You have to know that. Right?"

He said nothing. I could see his shape out of the corner of my eye as he drove us back. He had no more words and no answers for me. I didn't know whether to read that as agreement or disagreement. We drove on and on in silence as if neither response really mattered.

I finally brought myself to look at him. His eyes

were locked forward. They didn't look sad or angry. They didn't look like anything. His eyes were empty. There was no emotion behind them anymore. I wasn't sure if he had no feeling left for me or no fight left for our marriage. The well looked to be dry. He almost looked like he wasn't focused on anything. If he plowed into a tree and killed us both, maybe I would know for sure then. I wondered if we would both die in the car, but then wake up back in the house again anyway.

I smelled smoke thick in the car and it made me want to gag. I started to wonder if it was coming off of him instead of me. I was tempted to lean in and smell his clothes. That would have gotten a response one way or the other.

We were approaching the neighborhood with the nice old houses and our house which was just old.

How had it all come back to this house?

Foster had apparently fully given up trying to chat with me within a few minutes of picking me up, lost in his own dark thoughts. He hadn't bothered asking me what had happened which bothered me. I wondered if the police had filled him in or if he already knew somehow.

I turned to the property, but couldn't move my hand to open the door. My mind screamed to get out and run down the street and never stop, but I was frozen.

Foster frowned when it was obvious I wasn't getting out. At least he was showing some emotion.

I closed my eyes. I didn't want to argue. I didn't want to be with Foster in this house again. What had I really accomplished since the day I'd left? A slip into madness, a yearning to get high, constant money problems, and everything I had taken that I thought was important was now destroyed in a fire.

"Mom?"

Not everything.

I opened my eyes to see my girls standing in the driveway, waiting for me to exit the car.

Foster got out and slammed the door, scaring me. The car shook and the keys jingled where he left them in the ignition. I wondered if I should get them out for him.

I realized I was not only scared of the house; I was scared of my husband and what he might be capable of. I had the faint smell of smoke in my nostrils again right before he'd exited and I debated whose stink it was. We were both guilty in our own ways, but someone had set the fire and that detail mattered.

Maggie finally opened my door and hesitated before putting a hand out to help me. Her hair wasn't that bad. It was like a deep rose or a copper brown shade. I would have just let her do it. Her roots were showing through. I could have helped her do a better job. I could have helped, if I had been there.

Foster was already up the steps and into the house, the door slamming behind. If he was trying to tell me something, it was working: I was unwelcome.

I stood on shaking legs and the girls wrapped themselves around me, squeezing as tightly as they could. I missed this, even if it was under such horrible terms. So many fleeting moments of happiness with my girls swarmed in my head and threatened to knock me over. Haunted by past joys as painful in that moment as any loss.

Heather reached up and wiped a tear from my cheek I didn't know was there. I'd been crying so much lately it never registered.

"Are you coming in?" Maggie asked. I wondered if she'd be surprised if I told her no and got back into the car or just started walking away. I knew by the look on her face she wouldn't blame me.

"You need a shower," Heather said with a forced smile.

I did. I needed to shed the stink of the fire and wash away the dark mood I was in, but going inside was only going to add to it.

The girls led me by hand into the house. I didn't hesitate on the threshold, knowing it wasn't going to make it any easier if I fought it. I walked through the house and into the kitchen, keeping my eyes on the worn carpet and did not glance at the stairs leading to the upper levels. Foster's promise of scaffold, plastic, and renovation didn't make me feel better. It would be nothing more than dying hair. Eventually the roots were going to show again.

As I passed, I thought I heard a snicker. It might have been in my head. The girls didn't stop or seem to notice. I was truly going crazy being back in this house. I felt a chill like I'd never be able to go back out the front door again, except in a body bag.

I wanted a fix again. I wanted to get drunk and forget about life for awhile.

Foster was in the kitchen, but ran away through the other door like I was going to attack him. The girls led me to the kitchen table and helped me to sit.

"I'll get the bathroom ready for your shower,"

Heather said. She smiled faintly. "You can use Maggie's expensive shampoo and conditioner."

I turned my head as Foster swung back behind in the hallway and took the stairs up two at a time. Was it so horrible to be anywhere near me he'd chance going upstairs and dealing with the house?

Maggie poured me a glass of bottled water with no ice. I wanted nothing more from the house than I had to take and she knew this. I felt like the water and the ice made from the house's water would pollute me. It was part of the energy of this place that destroyed from the inside out. I even held my breath when taking a shower in this house and the last few weeks I'd been here I'd become more and more sure the house was trying to kill me.

"Did you and dad talk in the car?" Maggie asked.

I shook my head, but didn't offer anything else. We had said words. Would Maggie have understood that wasn't the same as talking? Foster was acting like he'd wanted to open up a dialogue with me at first I supposed, but his nervous energy pushed me away like a palpable force. He'd been like that in college at times when he was nervous and wanted to get something off his chest. I remembered when he'd proposed. He'd spent the night talking a mile a minute, his hands moving and his eyes darting so much I thought I'd get sick.

I supposed in my own way I had proposed to him on the way back here. I had proposed staying together as a family, if he was willing to leave. What a thing to ask of him. A proposal with conditions was not really true love, was it? Unconditional meant until death did us part, right? Sometimes not even then. Willing to die together was part of the contract. If you marry the guy, you marry his family and all the baggage that comes with that.

"We can't go on like this," she said but I didn't know who she was talking about. The entire family or just her and her sister? Somehow I knew she wasn't thinking of her father, who seemed resigned to staying in this place. No matter the cost.

I heard movement upstairs, but Maggie didn't budge, now seated at the table staring at me.

My little girl was growing up so fast. They both were. I felt like the worst mother in the world. I felt like I hadn't seen them in so long. When was the last time I'd sat down with them and had a one on one chat about life or boys or anything? I was so wrapped up in my own problems I didn't bother to see how they were holding up. Our last face to face had been me telling her to abandon her father and, when she wouldn't, I had left her here in this place and I had taken her sister. That moment was never going to leave her the way I had left her. My eyes burned worse than when I had been in the middle of the fire.

"Are you going to stay here?" Maggie asked. She was full of questions I didn't have the answers for or didn't want to share just yet. Truthfully, I had no idea what I was going to do after drinking this glass of water and taking a shower.

Heather joined us and sat across from me. We'd all taken our usual seats for dinner as if we hadn't skipped a beat. I knew Foster was too scared to join us.

"The bathroom is all yours," Heather said. She exchanged a quick glance with her sister and something dark passed between them. Since I'd been gone, the roles had changed, but I no longer knew where I fit in. I was a guest in my own house, even though it never was mine to begin with.

The floor creaked right overhead and we all tensed, but no one pulled their eyes to the ceiling. How many times had we done this over the weeks before I'd finally had enough?

Toward the end, we'd kept conversations going, talking over the noises and adding a couple of decibels to our own levels to drown some of it out. I remembered the night I'd finally broken and left...

Maggie handed me a napkin to dry my eyes. I was fully crying again. After drying my eyes a third time, I looked down and saw I had tied the napkin into a tight knot. I didn't remember doing it. Heather took the napkin out of my hand and balled it up.

I stood and stumbled to the bathroom, glad the girls didn't ask any questions or try to help me. I was broken inside, but not completely yet. I'd always been off, always had something wrong with me. I'd been lying to myself for too long.

When I stripped out of my dirty clothes and tossed them into the hallway before locking the door behind me, Maggie knocked lightly and told me she'd start the washer.

The shower was too cold and then too hot. Old pipes and an old water system in this old house. You could never get it just right unless it was the perfect temperature outside for several days in a row, which rarely happened in Georgia.

I stuck my head under and wondered if I drowned, would Foster even come downstairs to talk to the police. I washed my hair twice, still smelling the smoke afterward. I thought it was clinging to me on a molecular level. My body was scrubbed until the skin was so red it looked like a sunburn.

I felt eyes on me and pulled the curtain back so quickly and with so much force two of the hooks popped off.

There was no one there. Never was, even though I felt a presence. Watching me. It was such a violation to be spied upon when I was in the shower and even more vulnerable than usual.

"Leave me alone. Can't you give me one room to myself?" I whispered, an edge to my words. I wanted to strike out at something, but the bathroom was too ancient and too small. If I broke anything, the girls would come running. Not Foster.

It was only my imagination, but I suddenly felt alone again. As if telling an evil entity to leave really worked. I remembered a memory, as a small child, of being scared of monsters in the closet and someone telling me all I needed to do was shout I wasn't scared and for them to be gone. I'd done it and probably went right to sleep, none the wiser.

The world wasn't so black and white. This house was nothing but black to my family.

There was a knock at the door.

"Mom, I brought some of your clothes you left behind. Stuff I remember you wearing," Heather said through the closed door.

I smiled and wiped the mirror to see my old and haggard face.

"Thank you. Just leave it there and I'll get it in a second."

"Mom…"

I sighed. I didn't want a long, drawn-out conversation with a door between us. I knew Heather didn't want to look at me when she asked her barrage of questions, but I was just so tired right now.

"Yes, dear?" I finally asked and began toweling off. The bathroom was like a sauna and too cramped. I used to use the upstairs bathroom, which was large and bright and open. The full tub and shower you could throw a party in had been nice in the beginning.

"I'm, uh, well… I'm just glad you're here. I miss being with you and Maggie," Heather said.

Before I could answer I heard her walking away, the floorboards creaking.

I leaned against the sink and sighed. I knew I'd need to sit both of the girls down and explain a few things to them. My flight had been quick but not unexpected. If I could go back in time, I would have waited and taken them both with me when Maggie was ready to go, not that it did much in the long run. We were all still in this house.

I folded my towel and hung it on my hook like old times, falling quickly into the old habits. Since I'd been gone, no one had cleaned the bathroom and the toilet and tub had soap scum and rings. Maybe cleaning it would distract me for awhile. I wondered if I'd missed any work and if I still had a job. Where was my car?

My work uniforms were in the trailer. I realized my purse and ID and money and all of my clothes I'd taken were also gone. Even if my car hadn't been destroyed in the blaze, my car keys were lost in the fire. This was what it was like to feel stranded.

I opened the door and peeked out. I was alone. I could see into the kitchen and the girls had moved away from the kitchen table.

It was so cool in the hall. On days when the kids were at school and Foster was at work, I'd leave the bathroom door open during a shower so I could keep cool. I was also a little scared I'd open the door and see Hell.

Like old times, I started getting dressed. I chuckled when I saw the clothes she'd picked out for me: one of my old pair of blue panties that had too much wear, a pink bra with one of the straps torn, a pair of gray sweatpants I hadn't worn since I'd first met Foster but might still fit, and an Atlanta Braves t-shirt I'd gotten one Christmas from both girls.

Better times. Haunted by past joys.

I put the clothes on and adjusted as much as I could. I'd go find the rest of my clothes and trade out for something else as soon as Heather saw I was wearing what she'd picked out. I was actually feeling good about the sweatpants since I hadn't put on as much weight as I'd thought I had. The once-baggy pants were much tighter, but I could still move in them.

I looked up and caught a glimpse of someone watching me in the kitchen, but he moved too quickly to get a good look. I was sure it was Foster.

I looked down at the hairdryer under my hand. The cord had been knotted several times. That wasn't good for the cord, I thought. I decided not to dry my hair.

Chapter 12
MeLinda Goshen

"YOU'RE NOT SUPPOSED to keep alcohol in the home, Keith," I said.

I leaned my forehead against the door to the freezer. I could feel the cold escaping through the plastic from underneath like a ghost not quite being contained. The power was still on, so there was that. I wondered if the city would cut it after a couple bills were missed or if the police handled that. The police hadn't bothered locking the door, so I doubted they would handle anything else since all the evidence was either collected or ignored. I was part of the system that cleaned up family disasters, so if I didn't know, I figured maybe no one did. Of course, I was supposed to take the children out before they were dead and put them somewhere that they would not get hurt.

I failed. Now I was drinking the booze out of the fridge with power still on for whatever spirits haunted the address. I felt haunted.

I lifted the bottle to read the label. It was shredded onto the linoleum in crinkled strips where I had endlessly raked my thumb back and forth over it. I hated bottles with labels. I had drank all the hard stuff

– what I brought with me and what I found stowed in the crime scene of the Drake Street House where children were taken when they were in real trouble. Now I was down to Keith's shitty beer.

I cleared my throat, but brought up a wash of stomach acid. I swallowed it back down like my own brew of the hard stuff. Most of my stomach contents was alcohol at that point, so it wasn't far from the truth.

I said out loud, "If you are going to cheat, you should find someone hot, Keith. Don't fill your fridge with the bar skank of domestic beers."

I was both positive the alcohol had not been there when I did my last inspection and not the least bit sure at the same time. I'd do my best to get rid of it now. That was the least I could do.

The Walters kids' father was still in jail, where he went for child endangerment and for breaking my arm. I wondered when they were going to tell him his children were dead. I didn't know when that was done or how either. I had failed at my task, so I knew they didn't let the one that got the kids killed deliver the news. That was something generals did in wars. I was no general and, if this was a war, I was not winning or I was not fighting on the side I thought I was.

I stepped away from the fridge and walked back into the living room. I brought the skunky bottle up to my lips, but found my good hand empty. I must have dropped it. It had to be on the carpet or I would have heard it hit. I looked at my hand in the cast. Some co workers had signed the plaster of my cast with rough lined block letters like we were middle school girls. I saw the word hero scratched on the cast and my eyes stung with tears. I looked away from it, knowing I was carrying the mark on me like I was being mocked by dead eyes.

I felt like I needed to throw up. There were still bloodstains on the carpet and splattered dry and thick up along the walls. It made me think there had to be more than blood mixed in with it. It speckled the pictures of Keith and his wife hanging on the opposite wall. The walls were scarred around and between the dried specks of gore. Keith had taken after the walls when he ran out of flesh to stab. Then, he stabbed himself before the police could take him alive.

"Coward." As the word left my lips, I wasn't sure if I was talking about Keith or myself.

I wasn't sure who was supposed to clean up the blood. If everyone in the house was dead, I supposed it didn't really matter.

I saw something move in the shadows of one corner of the room. I cut my head over. I expected to see some teen couple that came in to screw before I got there and had been hiding. The room was splashed in blood. Horny teens would do it anywhere these days. If it wasn't teens, then a raccoon maybe. Neither. Nothing. It was just the ghosts I brought with me to join the ones I had made by being terrible at my job.

Spots moved over my vision. They were clear instead of black. It was like something swimming under a microscope between glass and plastic. I watched them move in and out of my line of sight like living things. I was pretty sure I was about to pass out.

I turned and Keith was sitting in the recliner

staring up at me. I threw up in my mouth again.

I gagged and said, "You are not here. I'm drunk."

Keith shrugged. Blood pooled in one of his dozens of wounds, soaking into his flannel shirt. He was bleeding from a couple spots on his neck, down into his collar. He had deep slashes on both sides of his throat. It looked like he had gotten both arteries. I didn't know that was possible for a person to do to himself.

His hand rested over a kitchen knife, balanced under the fingers of his right hand, with the point poking into the arm of the recliner, creating a dimpled crater in the material. He circled his hand around making the knife dance around erect.

He held my beer bottle with the missing label in the other hand.

"Mostly true," he said. Blood swelled up from his lips in bubbles. It gurgled in the back of his throat like he was congested. "I think I may be drunk too. I haven't felt right since everything went nuts, you know."

"Why did you kill everyone?" I asked my vision of Keith.

He rolled his eyes. They were sunken into his skull and the flesh around his sockets puckered, pale and shriveled.

He said, "The ones in the walls told me it would be over. They implied it. Somehow. I don't know. I really believed this was the way to make it all stop."

"Make what stop, Keith?"

He sniffed and something black oozed from one of his nostrils. Blood was seeping over the surface of his left eye like he had busted a blood vessel inside it.

115

"Harassment. The spirit world's version of Chinese water torture. Is that racist? I guess it doesn't matter now, huh?"

The Walters kids charged into the living room, screaming. I dropped to my knees and screamed back. I couldn't seem to stop. They circled the recliner and ran back into the wall, vanishing from sight. I clutched my chest and gasped. My heart was pounding until it hurt. I thought I was going to die on the spot and I wondered if I'd be stuck in a seat next to Keith.

"I'm losing my damn mind," I said.

"I know the feeling," Keith said. "There's more than that to lose, you know."

"Where did they go?" I asked staring at the spot on the wall where they had vanished.

"I don't know," Keith said. "They come and go. They talked about another house. I don't know where. They talked about an Uncle Duke Turner. Maybe they are able to go see family or something. Have to admit I'm a little jealous. Can't really say I've crossed over if I'm still parked in my same ass imprint in my same chair. My wife is in the bedroom. She hasn't spoken a word since I hurt her. Don't think she's going to forgive me, Linda. We may have forever and it might still not be enough time. I'm glad the kids don't look hurt anymore. I think maybe kids bounce back from this sort of thing faster than adults."

I wasn't hearing him entirely. What I was hearing, I wasn't exactly processing. All I managed to say to all that was. "Why'd you bring alcohol into the house, Keith?"

"Why did you, Linda?"

I breathed out. "To drown the ghosts."

"You just end up back in the same ass print. I can show you, if you're tired of living."

"Turner?" I stared at the wall. I shook my head. It hurt and made me feel dizzy. I was feeling foggy from being drunk. I was used to getting by on a buzz. I was a little past buzzed at that point, but the situation was calling for it, I thought.

I heard the springs in Keith's recliner groan and protest. I wasn't looking at him to see what he was doing. Maybe he was trying to get up. He could be getting another beer or putting the knife away.

I stood up and stumbled out the open front door. Keith's ghost shouted at my back, but I lost it in the haze of my plastered skull as I staggered across the lawn to the crappy Child Services car. I'd left the door open and the keys in the ignition. It was buzzing in a continuous note. Either the car was too shitty to steal or the neighborhood was a nice place to live. Used to be anyway. The ghosts of the slain are hidden behind closed doors with their coldness seeping out slowly through the wood, I thought.

I was surprised the battery wasn't dead. Everything else around here was. I got in and closed the door to get the noise to stop before my skull split.

My cell phone was on the passenger's seat where I'd left it. I had four missed calls from Drew and two from Gordon. Gordon knew how I thought, so I was worried he might show up here at any moment. That might be for the best. If I made him fire me, then I couldn't hurt anyone else, except myself.

But I started the car and put it into drive. I swerved over the middle line twice that I remember,

---

117

but I didn't remember much. I usually stayed close to the shoulder and drove obnoxiously slow when I was drunk, but I was seeing ghosts and had a broken arm

I got to the Turner house. My phone announced that I had arrived at my destination. I didn't remember starting the maps, but there was no other way I would have made that drive otherwise. I already had the address saved.

I sat in the driveway and stared at the bodies between me and the house. The sun did weird things to them. Some of them I could see through while others seemed more solid in the light. I saw the soaking wet woman again. I looked around for the Walters children, but did not see them among my ghostly lawn party. I wasn't going to get out of the damn car.

"Coward," I said.

Then, she came out. It was the girl I had met and taken earlier. Another child I moved from mom and sent home with dad. Usually went the other way. Maybe the other way was the right choice here. Maybe I needed to take both girls away and put them into another murder house. As I looked at the ghosts milling around, I thought maybe that was exactly what I had done here. Which choice was going to get her killed faster? I had no idea anymore.

Heather. Her name was Heather.

Heather Turner walked through the spirits without flinching and leaned into my passenger's side window. The fact she was acting like she didn't see them did not help my sense of sanity or my waning trust in my own judgment.

"Ms. Goshen?"

I swallowed. My throat burned. I felt like I was faking sober for an officer. I said, "Yes ... yes, Heather."

"My daddy is upstairs and he's in trouble. I need someone to go with me. My mother won't go because she's afraid. My sister won't go past the second floor because she doesn't trust the house anymore."

"Your mother is home, Heather?" Sometimes they accused each other of terrible things and then reconciled anyway. That didn't mean my job was over. Far from it.

"She came home with daddy after her trailer burned down."

Oh, shit. I glanced down at the missed call notices on my phone. What was happening to the world?

I said, "We need to call the police, if your dad is in danger or is ... if you are in danger here."

I was having trouble keeping my eyes focused anyway, but I kept looking past her at the bodies stretching out across the front of the house. If I was really imagining them or dreaming, I would expect them to fade in and out. I could stare at any one as he or she moved and never lose sight of them. It was like I was watching something real and right in front of me. It couldn't be real. Keith could not have been in that chair and children couldn't have come screaming in and out of the walls. But that's what Keith was screaming he saw with his last breath and now I was seeing and hearing it too.

Heather looked back at the house and said, "I don't think they will let the police in. They are able to touch and move things in the house. It makes them dangerous."

Oh, shit. I decided then that I would have felt better, if she had said something where I could pretend I was imagining it all. Then, I would be insane and the world would still be sane. That I could live with.

I thought about Keith holding the knife and my bottle. I thought I was imagining them, but could he touch the stuff? If he could touch the knife, then I was in there casually talking to a killer capable of using the knife again. The springs were protesting as he started to get up right before I left. What if I had stayed there on my knees a little while longer? I wasn't sure I was ready to decide any of this was real.

"Are the things in your house real? Are there real people, Heather?"

"My mom, sister, and dad are real. The others are real too, but I can't see them. My sister can, but she doesn't trust them anymore. Will you help me get my dad?"

If they wouldn't let the police do it, I wasn't sure why Heather thought I could do anything. I looked down at the word hero scratched on my cast. All I did was get children killed and get my bones broken. Insanity was sticking with plan A and hoping for outcome B this time. If the world was insane now, what else was there to do?

But I was drunk and self-destructive, so I opened the car door and left it buzzing, with the keys in the ignition and my phone on the seat.

Chapter 13
Ruthie Turner

MAGGIE HAD DRAWN the family when she was in kindergarten, me with my triangular skirt and circular hair, tiny Heather as a simple circle with two uneven eyes and Foster with his stick figure body and no real features. I wondered if it meant anything now as I stared at the drawing still on her wall. She'd brought it from her upstairs bedroom when the house started acting up.

Acting up. As if it were a child having a temper tantrum and not trying to kill us and add to the denizens of the place.

I sat down on her bed and wanted to sleep. I was exhausted and knew if my head came within inches of the soft pillow, I'd be out.

The front door opened. Maybe the girls had packed a bag while I was in the shower and escaped, never to be seen or harmed again. A mother could always hope.

I didn't have the energy to change my clothes just yet. I needed to formulate a serious game plan. Staying here wasn't an option, but I had no real money to stay at a hotel. I had nowhere to run to.

Foster would use this against me because he wanted me to stay in the house and keep the balance. He always talked about the balance as if this was a swimming pool and you needed the proper chemicals dumped in each day so children could swim in it.

Foster had wanted us to get a pool in the large backyard after the girls were born and started to get bigger. We certainly had the money then. The girls would have a fun place to swim and I could sunbathe and read Time magazine while watching them. Foster would come home from a hard day's work and cannonball into the water, splashing me before I knew what hit me.

He'd even had someone over to the house to do the measurements and get pricing. Everything had been set to go for the following month, but, at the eleventh hour, Foster came downstairs, sweating and wringing his hands, and told us we couldn't get a pool.

"It's just not very practical," he said to the girls.

When they protested, he got angry and cut them off with a wave of his hand.

"We can't go around digging up the yard. End of discussion," he'd said and stormed off. The pool was never brought up again and with so many other little things happening over time, it was another piece in the puzzle. It made sense to me right here in this moment why we never got the pool or did any other major renovations to the property: Foster had been told, by the powers that be, that we couldn't.

When I'd inquired about planting some flowers and/or a garden, Foster had gone upstairs and an hour later told me what spots on the vast property were best for me to do it.

There were no tire swings, no slide for the girls, no playing in the yard. Everything had been controlled from the moment we entered the house and now it was becoming crystal clear where I could and could not stand.

I went into the kitchen and opened the cabinet which used to house all of the snacks for the family. It was empty save for an opened box of Oreo cookies. Heather was famous for leaving things unsealed. I was sure the cookies were stale, which was a shame.

I was about to close the cabinet when I saw the hint of a bottle on the top shelf.

Had I left a bottle of alcohol in the house? Impossible. I was sober. I hadn't had a drink in far too long. Foster had kept any and all alcohol out of the house, always afraid I'd relapse. I knew at times he'd come home smelling faintly of mouthwash, but the Jack and Cokes he'd had still lingered. I remember kissing him fiercely at those times and I was sure he'd thought it was just about my yearning for the sex, but now I knew it was to get even a taste of the Jack in my system. I felt horrible and like I'd used Foster at times. I was so set on the fact he'd tricked me into this house and done all of these horrible things that forced me to flee, but in the end I was also a rotten wife and person.

I sat down at the kitchen table. The noises upstairs were now silent, but I knew someone or something was listening to my heartbeat. I wanted to call out for the girls, but decided against it. I wasn't ready to talk just yet.

The front door opened again and closed seconds

later. I heard the floors creak as whoever it was came walking toward me.

I wanted to flee at that moment. I didn't want to deal with either of my daughters and especially Foster. Right then I felt like a real jerk when it came to him, even though it wasn't all my fault. I knew it also wasn't all his fault, which I'd been using to get me through the days.

Heather came into the kitchen with a concerned look on her face that turned to anger. She threw her hands in the air.

"Seriously, mom? Are you friggin' kidding me?" Heather stormed out of the kitchen and into her bedroom, slamming the door so hard the plates in the cabinet rattled.

She hadn't been alone. The social worker, Miss Goshen, was standing in the kitchen doorway.

"Mind if I join you?" she asked.

I shrugged my shoulders. I was done running away from her. I had nowhere else to go. I had the horrible feeling she'd think I'd torched my trailer or tried to kill myself. Had I tried to end my life?

"You pouring or me?" she asked.

It was then I realized why Heather had been so mad and stomped away.

There was a three-fourth's full bottle of Jack Daniels Honey and two glasses on the table in front of me. I didn't remember pulling the bottle off of the shelf and definitely didn't open up the other cabinet to get glasses down.

Something thumped above our heads, but Miss Goshen didn't seem to hear it, staring at the bottle on the table.

"Miss Goshen…"

"Please, call me Melinda." When I didn't move to open the bottle, she took it in her trembling hands.

"Melinda, I guess we need to talk," I said. It was better to go on the offensive than to get riddled with questions I might not want to answer or know how to answer. "I had nothing to do with the fire. You have to believe me. I woke and everything around me was ablaze."

Melinda poured generously from the bottle into both glasses and slid one closer to me with a finger. Her eyes stayed on the bottle. I started twisting a napkin around my fingers.

"I'm not here for that. I didn't even know about it until your daughter told me," she said.

"I know I should've kept in touch. I'm sorry. You have to understand what's been going on," I said and unconsciously looked at the ceiling. I knew I was playing a dangerous game by being so open, but I was desperate. Maybe she could help me and the girls get out while we still had a slim chance.

She took a sip of the whiskey and sighed.

"I had my arm broken recently when I tried to get kids out of a dangerous situation. Single father mixed up in stuff. Girlfriends in and out of the house. Neglect. Accusations of other stuff," she said, and held up her cast a few inches. "He's in jail and his kids ended up dead where I tried to put them. I had a conversation with the man who did it, too."

"That's horrible," I said.

"You don't know the half of it." She took another sip and finally looked away from the bottle and directly at me. "He's dead."

I looked up again.

"He and his wife had taken care of kids from emergency placements, for us, for years. He and his wife were good we thought. Three children. Lovely. He killed them all as well as his wife. A small detail about it all, but it stuck in my head. The odd thing about this, and as you can see, I'm already well past odd and into certifiable, is the birth mother's maiden name. Turner."

I couldn't breathe.

She poured more whiskey into her glass. "I probably wouldn't even have remembered, but shortly after the third kid was born years ago, she walked out of the house in the middle of the night and died face down in a retention pond. No sign of struggle. Maybe postpartum. It caught my attention as I was investigating the father. Turner … and then Keith, the killer, mentioned it. He talked about an Uncle Duke."

My eyes went to the glass in front of me, a scant few inches from my reach. I was always a fan of whiskey. Hell, I was a fan of anything that took me out of my head and my thoughts.

"Uncle Duke lived here. He raised Foster when he was younger. After his parents... after what happened." I didn't feel right saying aloud what had been done in the past. I didn't like talking in this kitchen with the house listening.

"Where is Uncle Duke now?" she asked.

"Long gone."

"Funny but up until a few hours ago I would have thought a statement like that meant something. Now I'm not so sure," she said and took another sip.

"I never met him. I'm trying to wrap my head around far worse things right now," I admitted. I touched the glass with my pinkie.

"With everything I've screwed up lately, I doubt I have a job anymore," she said and finished the whiskey in her glass.

She glanced at my glass, still untouched, before pouring herself another two fingers worth.

"Why are you here?" I asked.

She shrugged. "A dead man told me his case was somehow related to your case. I can't wait to explain this in a report. When I pulled up, your youngest said your husband was in trouble and you were back home."

"We're all in trouble being in this house," I said. "He's upstairs, but I wouldn't go and find him. I don't… I can't go up there. It isn't safe for anyone."

"Why did you come back? Do you know how cliché it is you returned to your husband? Frankly, I thought you'd be better than the rest and beat the odds," she said.

"It has nothing to do with my husband," I said defensively. I was going to argue about the trailer burning being the only reason I had come back, or the vulnerable daughters I'd left behind, or a dozen other excuses. But were they valid?

I felt like I needed stability, even if it was harmful. I'd traded drugs and alcohol chaos for this house.

I pushed the whiskey away and Miss Goshen followed it with her eyes like a cat staring at a jumping piece of yarn.

"Foster is upstairs with everyone," I said. I felt

like I needed to work through some things, but it was becoming a bit clearer. In order to protect my daughters, I needed to stay and comply with whatever came. My life was forfeit in order for them to somehow escape this madness.

Would the house let me trade my life for their safety? I didn't matter anymore. I was just the pawn to trade for precious lives.

I grabbed the glass just as Melinda put her hand up to get it.

The whiskey burned going down my throat, but it was a deliciously good sensation. It was like an old friend and we'd picked up the conversation right where we'd left off after all these years.

Melinda looked crestfallen even though there was still whiskey in the bottle.

"I think it's almost time to go upstairs and introduce you to the Turner family," I said.

She was half-listening as she grabbed the bottle and poured half of the remaining whiskey into her glass.

I held up my glass and she topped me off.

"I'm scared of going upstairs," she said.

She wasn't the only one.

When the man who'd frightened me at work the other day stepped into the kitchen doorway behind Melinda with a cigar between his lips and a knowing smile, it hit me.

This was Uncle Duke.

My life had just gotten harder.

I tried in vain to keep the glass from falling from my hand as I passed out and fell out of the chair.

Chapter 14
Foster Turner

I CAME BACK to myself staring down a monochrome hallway. It was like I was looking at a black line drawing of a hallway. Some art student was studying perspective and was practicing with hallway sketches. I had wandered, barefoot again of course, past the strip clubs and warehouses to this hipster's sketch book.

As my synapses settled, I started to see shadings come into focus in brown tones. There were exposed nails. Boards folded up from the braces underneath exposing blackness. The world was shadow underneath the sketches. I knew that from an early age.

Something alive crawled up out of the darkness with a lazy, dodgy pattern, from side to side, like its tiny insect brain couldn't decide on a course. Maybe I shouldn't assume everything I saw moving was actually alive. I should have learned that lesson a long time ago too. It wasn't a roach I recognized. It had a bulbous black back like it was swelling up from eating too much darkness. The exoskeleton was nearly a hemisphere making me think some rare desert beetle had wandered in. Jesus, had I gotten on a plane and flown barefoot to Egypt or Libya?

The hallway wasn't dry though. Water puddled around the low points in the warped boards and seeped into the open spaces. The whole structure might give way one day. Maybe today was that day with my weight on the boards. The ceiling spotted with mold and greenish-gray growth. The plaster bubbled and puckered in warts and pockmarks like the face of the survivor of some disfiguring pox. The doors on both sides of me tilted on their hinges within the frames. I wasn't sure any of them would open even if I did want to see what was inside. I wanted to find stairs or an exterior door and find my way to a sign that told me what part of the Earth I was on.

One of them stepped through a door without opening it. As she tore through the flat, splintered surface, the door rattled in its frame. The hardware around the loose knob clinked as it bounced with the disturbance. The door held again like nothing had happened. She crossed the hall on the diagonal. Her hair was wet and stringy. Her nightgown clung to her in profane ways. I could see the shapes of ribs and withered breasts underneath. Duke had told me her name once or twice. He had even hinted to me who she was and how we were related. I was still in high school, I think, the first time I saw her. Maybe I was older. There were a lot of faces to remember. I let most of them, living and dead, go.

I never quite got my mind back straight after the loss of my parents, so the information didn't stick. That's when I could start seeing people like the soaking wet woman. My father and mother bleeding out flipped that particular spiritual switch in my brain among others. I lost a lot of information after that, in the darkness behind the sketches that covered over the pitch black reality of life. It went the same way as all my parents' friends that asked if I was okay, if there was anything I needed, or if I just needed to talk. I didn't remember their names either and they were gone like spirits vanishing in the sunlight. I wish ghosts really left when the sun came up.

Duke had told me her name and that she was harmless. Well, he had actually said mostly harmless, winked, chewed his cigar, and took a swig of martini. She pushed into the surface of another door with only the slightest pop from the frame. Beads of moisture stood on the surface in a rough shape of her body. The air was moist and I was guessing there was a temperature difference involved too.

I narrowed my eyes and looked to the side. I saw shreds of the wallpaper folded down away from the wall and coiled at the edge of the wide base boards. I was in the house. I looked up at the rotting ceiling. Rotting, wet ceiling meant bad roof and the attic was probably a putrid mess. It must have been like trying to breathe methane up there. And the furniture, clothes, and papers stored up there would be destroyed. There was an A frame joist system and oaken master beams. Much of the weight of the house was supported from above. My father had explained it to me once, back when he was alive, before he cut out his own tongue, among other things.

The wet weight of the ruined items up there pulling on the spongy flooring was going to bring the whole house down. It had been a very long time since

I had come up here. I wouldn't have come up now if I was in my own mind. It was hard to believe I ever slept up here as a kid. I couldn't believe Duke hadn't told me about the roof. It seemed odd that he wouldn't have me move things to try to save them and repair the place.

I stared at the dying ceiling and realized they would not want me to move things they could still touch and lift. The things they could still feel from their lives would be things they would hold on to desperately, even if it meant those things slowly crumbled into nothing in the process. They were going to do the same thing to my girls – my three girls counting Ruthie – and I was helping them to do it. I shouldn't have helped this house against Ruthie, but they couldn't make me do anything I didn't want to do somewhere deep down.

I wanted a damn drink. That was in the cabinet in the kitchen. I had poured one out, but then another showed up the day I brought in the scaffolding and plastic. Shit, Ruthie was downstairs too. Wasn't she? I couldn't remember. I should have been down there. Nothing was stopping her from grabbing both girls and running. Maybe I needed to be away to let that happen. But deep down I wanted them all here with me. I wanted them with me and the house wanted me here, so it was all headed down the same drain. After all Ruthie had been through, was I really the worst thing that happened to her?

I tried to remember when I had lost time. I was driving with Ruthie from the hospital. I told her about Maggie's hair. Then, darkness. I thought Ruthie had started to say something, but I remembered none of it.

For all I knew, Duke had me leave her in a ditch somewhere. But he wouldn't do that because he wanted her here. He wanted us all here.

Now that I knew where I was, I looked down the color starved hallway and I realized which room I was facing at the end. I stared at the closed door and the entire scene pulsed once in my vision. Everything moved forward a millimeter before popping back out to what I thought of as real life. It had to be a pressure change. Probably behind my eyes. I wondered how much blood pressure had to change to shift a person's vision in an instant. The perspective changed for me so that I felt like all I could see was that damn door at the end of the hall and everything else seemed smaller and less focused. I knew that was all mental pressure and had nothing to do with blood.

"It has everything to do with blood," I said. I was hoping I was speaking to myself, but this was the kind of house where one could not be alone – especially not on the third floor.

I did not want to go to that room. Of course, they could not make me go anywhere I didn't really want to go and here I was facing it. None of the others liked going through that door either. How bad does a place have to be to haunt the dead? That room was the answer. At least I knew my father wouldn't be in there. If I was going to get permission to save my children or to free Ruthie, it was going to come from in there.

"Mister, do you live here?" a voice said from behind me – directly behind me.

I startled and jumped forward several steps before turning around. I didn't even bother to look down for nails first. Maybe I would end up with tetanus and lockjaw. I wasn't sure I wanted to see what my spirit would look like up here, if I died from that. My father had cut out his own tongue.

It was a young boy. He looked younger than my girls. He had no decay or blood on him. He was new maybe or not from the third floor. I hadn't seen him before, of that I was sure. I could almost believe he was alive and wandered in the house, if I had been anywhere else.

"What?" I said.

"I couldn't find Duke," the boy said.

My throat went dry. "Did he bring you here?"

If he brought you, will he bring my girls one day? Did he only keep me alive because he needed one living Turner in the house? I left those questions unasked.

"I don't know," the boy said. "I can't remember. It's been hard to think. But we were watching a woman and she got out. Now I can't find Duke."

I started to ask another question, but then stopped. I licked my lips. "What woman?"

The boy looked away and scrunched up his face. I got the impression that were there any blood flowing through him, he would be blushing. He said, "The one in her underwear."

I started to ask what color, but then I realized it really didn't matter. Had Duke brought her here too? I remembered him crashing the car and then I was on my way to pick up Ruthie. I remembered driving toward the house and then nothing. I didn't even know for sure if the girls were still here or not.

I wished I remembered the whole drive home with

her. I tried to talk to her. I tried to talk to her about anything. Her barriers were up too high. I was the enemy now and she was keeping me out. Duke must have taken the wheel and he had a tendency to crash cars.

"Take me to her. Don't go through walls. We have to use the halls."

He tilted his head, "You aren't like us?"

I swallowed and said, "Not yet anyway. You probably want to stay off the third floor as long as you can, kid."

Chapter 15
Melinda Goshen

WHEN SHE TOOK the drink, I felt like I was dying a little inside. With everything else that was happening, it was a tiny death by comparison. Foster had said she was an addict. A lot of husbands made accusations when custody fights started. She hadn't touched the glass I had poured her until that moment though. I had been reaching for it to take it for myself and then she downed it. I was the enabler this time.

In true form, I poured her another. She had been knotting up napkins the whole time we were talking. There were five she had done up during our conversation. The fifth one looked oddly like a noose. That wasn't a brand of origami I was familiar with, but I could get behind the sentiment.

The guy with the cigar walked in. I thought it was Foster at first. It took me a moment to remember I had already met Foster the night I returned Heather in the rain. This was not him. This stranger wore a floppy hat like he planned to go fishing. Maybe fishing in the fifties. Green shirt and khaki pants. The wrapping on the cigar was unraveling. It dropped to the floor of the kitchen like dead flesh falling off a corpse. The cigar was old and not stored well.

Ruthie fell out of her chair, into a heap on the floor, spilling her second glass over the edge of the table. Two of her knotted napkins sopped up the spill. The others scattered to the floor with her. That was one way to break a good drinking habit. I couldn't have a drinking buddy that went under the table after one. I wanted to catch her, but somehow I couldn't bring myself to move. I might not be far behind her, I decided.

He started talking like nothing out of sorts had happened. "I like this. Two ladies in the downstairs kitchen drinking in the middle of the day. It is like old times again. Granted, you two are dressed more like twelve year old scamps instead of proper ladies and the choice of drink is a little scandalous. Truth is, women didn't hold their drink very well back then either. That's what all those vapors and afternoon naps were about."

"Who the hell are you?" I asked.

"So unladylike," he said. "How did you end up here? I thought you had gotten put out to pasture."

"How do you even know who I am?" I asked.

"How do you think?" he shouted. "What are you doing here? Don't you have other messes to clean up? Tell me."

"Are you Duke Turner?"

He narrowed his eyes at me. For a moment, I saw the flesh around his eyes come loose and begin to crinkle. I thought his face was going to fall off like the cigar wrapper. His eyes darkened. I don't mean in the emotional sense. It wasn't the marbled black from horror movie monster's eyes either. It was a darkness that felt more real and less dramatic. Then, his eyes were back to being alive and his face was back attached and smooth. "How would you know that?"

"Keith told me."

Duke's dying cigar dipped downward between his lips. He tilted his head and a single string of hair flopped over from the pile on top of his head. The details were too specific to be a vision. He was not how I imagined any ghost, if that is what he was. "Who in rogue's goddamned gallery is Keith and why does he know me?"

I wanted to see his reaction. It was the only reason I answered. I thought his face might actually come off. Maybe his imaginary flesh would slough right off his borrowed bones. I was just drunk enough to want to see it. I spoiled for a fight when I was wasted. I said, "Keith was the group home dad where the Walters kids were murdered. Apparently his ghost is still haunting the recliner in the house where he murdered everyone. The kids keep running back and forth through the walls between there and a house with Uncle Duke Turner, who I am guessing is you. I remembered their birth mother was a Turner and drowned facedown in a pond years ago. As long as I was seeing ghosts, I figured I should come and see what was haunting this place."

"Birth mother? Is that what the baby daddies call them these days?" Duke shook his head losing more layers of cigar. "Unbelievable. I told everyone to wait to deal with that, but you were a problem and we needed to stir up your world a little – give you bigger fish to fry. Here you are anyway. You are like a broken down Sherlock Holmes with the lady parts.

How unfortunate for you."

I wasn't sure if he meant being a woman was unfortunate or my snooping around was going to lead to an unfortunate end. I thought about the knife on the arm of Keith's chair and the cigar in Duke's chops. What else could he throw around in this kitchen? I glanced over at the knife block on the counter. It was missing a few. In the dishwasher, I hoped. I turned my attention back on him hoping I hadn't given him any ideas.

"Were you the voices in the walls driving him insane until he killed them all?"

"I had other chores actually. Others took on that job. You know she killed herself to keep from killing her kids. So many mothers reach that point and drive right into the water with the kids with them, but she had the iron to take herself down to save them. After enough time though, she wanted them with her and she went with the others into your buddy Keith's walls to get her kids back. We are all driven to draw family closer to us forever. Like the drive to create life. The drive to take it. The drive to drink."

I looked over at the bottle, closer to the seat Ruthie had vacated. It was just out of my reach. I wanted another though. "I think I've had enough."

"I've heard that before," Duke said and snorted. "That's another odd thing. With most folks, drinking tears down barriers. We think it is the booze, but, when you see things from my perspective, you realize we let them down ourselves and the demons in the bottle just whisper the permission. Usually, drink helps us move things along and get the latest generations to do what we want them to do. You are the opposite. You are the rare breed of filly that seems to put more barriers up the more drunk you are. You must have been a lousy date. I've been trying since you crossed our lawn to get inside your skull. You are nothing but barriers though. Behind it all, I'm not even sure you actually want anything. Deep down, I don't think you even really want to help the people whose lives you meddle in. Can't do much with someone that wants nothing. I'm not much of a fan of wild cards either, filly."

"Maybe you just aren't a fan of women in general, Duke," I said.

He stared at me before taking the blasted cigar out of his mouth. He bent forward where his hat covered his eyes just a little and spit out loose tobacco from between his lips. When he went back up straight, I expected to see darkness in place of eyes, but normal human peepers still stared out at me.

"A bachelor of a certain age, you mean?" he said. "We get used to going on the way we got on. You know what? She is still soaking wet after all this time, right to the very day she finally brought her kids back home."

I looked down at Ruthie sprawled out on the floor at my feet. I thought about Heather coming home wet. Ruthie came home from a fire. Was she wet from the hoses? She wasn't wet as I looked down on her on the kitchen floor, even with the spilled glass of whisky next to her. He said she was still wet after all this time and brought her kids home. After a couple beats, I realized he was talking about the Walters kids. Their mother had died in a pond in the middle of the night and then screamed at Keith from the walls until he

140

killed them all. I remembered the soaking wet woman on the road in a nightgown and my heart skipped a beat. I wasn't sure it was going to restart.

"You are drunk and you can see us," Duke said. "That's usually the magic combo. We can work with that on most bitches, filly. See, Ruthie cleaned up which lowered her tolerance for the stuff, but raised it against us. She kept us out that way too. But she is wired for the fall now."

Something crashed loud enough upstairs that I thought the ceiling was going to come down on us. Two more bumps followed.

Duke looked up too. "God, an old house and old family like this, I spend all my time fixing one thing or another. Ruthie, we have shit to do. Wake up, girl."

Ruthie blinked and sat up. She used my chair to balance as she regained her feet. I reached out to try to steady her, but then she wrapped her hands around my throat. As I fought against her wrists with my one good hand, she wasn't even really looking at me. I tried to hit her with my cast, but only got a glancing blow on her shoulder. It hurt like hell in my arm even though I was loaded. I leaned out and tried to grab the whisky bottle, but ended up knocking it over on its side on the kitchen table.

"Mom? Mom?!"

As I was still leaned out to the side in my chair looking past Ruthie's body, I saw a girl I didn't recognize. My mind tried to make it Heather, but it wasn't. The world was blurring out and I had no idea if she was alive or not.

"Make her stop," the girl said from a great distance. "I brought her back like you said. Stop

---

141

making her do this. Stop it now."

"This is family business. Go play with your dolls or something." Uncle Duke lifted his pitiful cigar between his fingers and brought it back to his lips.

Chapter 16
Ruthie Turner

KILL, KILL, KILL...

The mantra played in my head as I tried to adjust my eyes. I was between conscious and unconscious thought, but it sounded like I was on a stage, the crowd echoing back like a cheer over and over.

Kill, kill, kill...

It was strength to me and I wanted more. Now I knew what it felt like to be a rock star, to be a pro athlete, to be someone important who the masses cherished and goaded to do more and more for their own amusement.

The extended family was surrounding me, all eyes on my hands as I blinked into focus.

My hands were throttling Miss Goshen.

Maggie was trying in vain to break my grip, my nails digging into the woman's skin and drawing blood. My fingers were so tense they hurt from the pressure of trying to choke the life out of the woman. Her eyes rolled around in her head like marbles spinning on a tabletop and I wondered what they'd sound like when they fell to the floor.

"Mom, you're killing her," Maggie said and tried punching my arms to break the death grip. It wasn't going to work. I was going to kill this woman because... why?

Kill, kill, kill...

Uncle Duke leaned forward, taking the cigar from his mouth and pointing with it. "You're almost there, Ruthie. Finally, welcome to the family."

I had a quick vision of Maggie, in complete panic mode like she sometimes did when she thought she'd misplaced homework or forgotten to study for a test, running around the kitchen.

Her hair wasn't that bad. She just needed to touch up the roots. Now that I was home, I could help her with that kind of stuff again. I could help. I could fix it.

I used to work a second job, at a diner near Douglasville, before Foster and I were married. It only lasted a few months, but I'd made a few friends and the owner took a shine to me. For our wedding gift from the diner, he gave me one of his thick, old school frying pans. I had to lift it with two hands when it was filled with food, but it was magical when I used it to cook. I know it sounds funny, but food just tasted better when I used it.

Maggie used it now to club me on the side of the head to get me to loosen my grip on Miss Goshen's throat.

THERE WERE BODIES in the yard. I was sure of it.

I woke with a start, expecting to be on the kitchen floor. Instead I was lying on the couch in the living room with a bag of melting ice on my temple and the water dripping down, trying to get into my mouth. Water from this house. I sat up and threw the ice bag on the coffee table.

I was alone. I'd expected the girls to be hovering or at least Duke to be sitting in the chair across from me.

The house was holding its breath like I was. I stood and the pain was unbearable. The side of my face felt like it had been caved in. My jaw hurt. My little girl had given me a shot I wouldn't soon forget. I couldn't blame her, of course.

Was everyone upstairs? Had something really bad begun without me? Did Duke think I was too much of a wild card for his nefarious plans?

I needed to leave. I walked to the front door and turned the handle, expecting to get shocked or the door to be sealed shut. It opened easily like it always did.

I stepped outside into the Georgia heat and the glare gave me an even bigger headache. The street was a hundred feet from where I stood and it looked like freedom. I had nowhere to run to. What if I went to the police and told them what happened?

Excuse me, officer, I choked a woman to death, but the ghosts in the haunted house forced me to.

I walked around to the side of the house. The warped and rusting shed seemed to be staring back at me, two rips in the metal looking like eyes.

There was a shovel to the left as I opened the door with a screech, birds in the trees squawking in annoyance.

If I had to, I would dig up the lawn to find what I knew was already there: the bones of the Turner generations.

I walked to the back of the house and looked around. My thoughts and semi-dreams hadn't really been specific. There was no 'dig to the east of the oak tree six paces out' or anything resembling an X marking the spot.

I decided fifty feet from the back porch was a good enough place to start.

As I raised the shovel and plunged it into the soil, I felt someone watching me.

I turned to see Duke, standing in the open back doorway, shielding his eyes from the sun.

"Come inside, Ruthie. You're wasting your time. There's nothing out here, and even if there was, it would take a backhoe to figure it all out," he said. "There's still some whiskey."

Bastard. I went back to the lawn, furiously turning topsoil over with the shovel. It produced nothing but soil and rocks.

"Last chance before I dump it down the sink,"

Duke said.

"I'm not listening to you, Duke. You can't hurt me anymore," I said.

I heard him laugh. "Are you sure about that? There are many more ways to hurt someone than to simply hit them or stab them or shoot them, you know? The pain of losing a loved one hits a deep vein."

I turned, angry, but my eyes were drawn to a third story window.

Xandra, terror etched on her face and only wearing her underwear, was slamming her fists so hard on the glass they were bleeding. The window wasn't budging. The house was too strong now.

"What have you done?" I asked.

"I'm only doing what needs to be done. What's been set into motion. You act like this is all my doing, but I'm as much a pawn in it as you are, Ruthie." Duke lifted his gaze up. "Your trailer park trash friend is just in the unlucky spot of being in the wrong place at the wrong time."

There was nothing I could do for Xandra right then. I knew she was the ploy to get me back into the house. She might already be dead and part of the problem, too.

I went back to digging, but it was slow going. The ground was filled with rocks only a few inches underneath, as if I was cutting through a giant's skin and hitting his skull.

"Ruthie, there's nothing out here anymore. It's all been moved. Foster's parents got nosy, too. We had to move the bodies to a safer location. We had to keep them from being disturbed again," Duke said.

"I don't believe you," I said and kept digging, walking a few feet to the left and striking.

"Whether you want to believe me or not, we're on the same side. You married into this mess and produced two beautiful and intelligent offspring," Duke said.

I turned, wishing he were closer so I could bash his head in with the shovel.

"You stay away from my girls," I yelled.

Duke shrugged. Any semblance of him trying to be nice was just an illusion. He'd been trying to butter me up and sucker me to come inside.

"I'm not coming back into the house. Ever," I said.

"Too bad. I didn't want to make this any harder than it had to be. I was being sincere when I talked about your girls. They could've made a difference, but you're changing the rules. Ever hear the expression *house rules*?" Duke put the cigar back into his mouth.

I looked back up to see Xandra, still bleeding as she tried to punch her way out.

Then it hit me.

The third floor was the concentration of evil. Always had been. Why?

Because the bodies were there. All of them.

As well as Maggie and Heather, who appeared at another window on the floor and waved for me to stay back.

Chapter 17
Maggie Turner

I STOOD OVER my mother with the pan. She went to her knees next to the woman in the chair.

The woman in the chair had red rings and bloody scratches around her neck where my mom's hands had been. I expected bruises. Maybe bruises took longer. The woman's eyes rolled up to the whites and her head lulled back. Veins stood out bumpy and gross around her skull. She smelled like she had been drinking cleaning products or bathing in rubbing alcohol. Maybe she peed herself from being choked.

A bottle lay turned over on the table. It was one with the squared sides, so it didn't roll as the liquid glugged out of the mouth onto the floor. It sounded like someone pissing with a blockage or the noise diarrhea makes. I couldn't remember ever seeing alcohol in the house when my parents were together. I looked at the squared bottle like it was an intruder. This was something alien in our home splashing out piss colored drink.

Mom pitched forward and collapsed on her face on the floor. I thought I might have killed her. The left eye of the woman my mother had been choking spread with a swirl of red as blood filled in the white from something busted down underneath the eye. I thought my mom may have killed her. I expected to see their ghosts standing together looking around at their own bodies, confused like they were in some old cartoon.

I didn't know where to start, so I dropped the pan with a clatter. It splashed up some of the cold whisky piss onto my leg below my capris.

I ran across the kitchen and started opening up drawers without closing them back. There were knitted hot pads, seasonal pot holders, utensils that were rarely used like the cheese grater and something for hand juicing fruit. I knew which drawers had the stuff I needed if I stopped and thought about it, but there was no time to stop and think.

I opened the drawer with the plastic bags finally. It had a shopping bag from Kroger with other shopping bags balled up inside. There was a nearly empty box of sandwich bags. We would need more soon. I thought I should put those on the list once I was done with this. I yanked out one of the gallon freezer bags.

I turned and saw Duke standing between me and the refrigerator. He was wearing an all white suit that looked like something sewn together from old bed sheets with buttons stitched on. His hair looked a little windblown. That made no sense to me. Why should any of this have made sense though?

"Get out of my way, dick," I said.

"You going sailing with that mouth, Captain?" he asked.

"Your cigar looks stupid."

I walked forward without slowing down and went

right through him. It was like staring through smoke until I came out on the other side. I felt the bag drag in my hand slightly. It was like I had caught a little of him in it on the way through. I actually looked in the empty bag expecting to see a ghost hand or a kidney, but it was empty just like before. It hurt a little. My skin ached and I felt prickles of heat. I didn't know if any of that was real, but I didn't plan on trying it again.

I opened the freezer and started raking cubes out of the ice maker into the bag.

I couldn't help myself from looking back over my shoulder at Duke. He looked legitimately ruffled from the experience. He set his cigar down on the counter next to the coffee maker.

"I saw a few bar fights in my day," he said, "but when a couple momma cats start fighting, there ain't nothing like it. Do you see what you did to her, Captain? Frying pan, hot damn. That sounded off her skull like a Chinaman's gong."

"You made her do it," I said, as I closed the freezer and fought the plastic zipper to seal the bag of ice. "And you made me have to do it too. I should have never listened to you."

"Can't make anyone do anything they don't already –"

"Shut up." I yelled.

I ran to her side and tried to lift her. Mom's joints felt like a string puppet with the strings cut. She felt heavy in weird places. I lowered her back down on her face and set down the bag of ice.

As I tried to catch my breath, I saw that the woman slumped in the chair was still breathing, but was out cold with her eyes open. One eye was blood red.

"They both got it good," Duke said as I was trying to catch my breath. "My dad and his brothers used to practice fighting. They figured out if you hit someone just right on the neck, up on the artery, you could knock them out. They practiced until they could do it with one shot each. They got in a real fight and one shot to the neck knocked my dad and his brothers out. They weren't getting better at hitting. They were getting attuned to being knocked out. Most of them died of aneurisms when they were older and always wondered if it was from damaging that artery when they were stupid kids. You got to be careful knocking folks out."

"I'd like to knock you out," Maggie said.

"You know you're named after Margaret Mitchell, the woman that wrote that torrid book about the War of Northern Aggression?" Duke said.

"Unless you're going to help, shut up."

"I'm always helping, Captain. Never stop. Never."

I rolled my mom over to her back and lifted her by her shoulders. As I dragged her feet across the floor with her head against my body, I was afraid I was going to drop her. I considered getting Heather to help, but I didn't want her to see this.

"You should have let her finish with the filly there, Captain. This was adult business and children are meant to be seen, not heard," he said.

I rolled my mom up onto a couch and ran back into the kitchen. "You had no problem with me when I was doing your dirty work for you."

"I do appreciate that. The whole family does. Those of us that stay behind bear the extra responsibility of those that abandon their families."

I picked up the ice and ran back to my mother's side. I put it on the lump I could already see forming on her head. "Mom, can you hear me?"

"People think they can run from family, but that's how they really end up haunted," Duke said standing over my shoulder as I stroked my mother's cheek to try to get her to come around. "Hell of a thing splitting up a family. They drag the spirits with them. Divide the family's power and history. The living battle over property and split it up or sell it not thinking about how that scatters the souls of people that invested their whole lives in it. What we keep and what we throw away has consequences beyond the life we can see. Everything that haunts us is driven by the weight of all the spirits that came before – generations of weight. Why people drink, why they use opiates, why they read poetry, why they kill themselves, why they kill loved ones, and why they screw is all a reaction to how we respect or disrespect what came before us."

"Why are you telling me this?" I asked.

"You should learn from your elders," he said. "Learn respect."

I shook my mother by her shoulder again. "Maybe we can share a nice silence, Duke."

"You are a clever one," Duke said, "Where did I put my cigar?"

"It's a dirty habit," I said. "It'll kill you one day."

"So, clever," he said, still patting his pockets. I wondered if he could actually keep anything in his pockets. "Your namesake had some dirty habits too, you know."

"What are you talking about?" I stood up straight with the moisture from the ice running along my mother's face. It was like cold tears. Where had my dad gone? What should I do about Heather and the woman in the chair? Would calling an ambulance make it worse? I needed to get my family away from this place and the things in it. My mother had tried and failed. Maybe I should have helped her when I had the chance.

Duke said, "I'm talking about Margaret Mitchell, the harlequin romance writer from down the road. I had an older cousin that used to go by Margaret's house on her way to the park with her girlfriends. Old Margaret used to show kids dirty picture books she had collected. I never saw them myself, so all this is hearsay, but I heard it from my sister and she was not one for telling stories out of church. Margaret was celebrated for being liberated and running with wild kids like the Teddy boys and girls. She got into high end erotica later and was celebrated for it. It was a fun little tidbit to tell about that writer from Atlanta, but it all started with her dirty picture books."

I stared at him for a moment and then walked around him to go back through the kitchen. The chair was empty. The spilled bottle was gone from the table. "Where did she go?"

"Damn it." Duke growled. "See. You got me telling stories and the whole place is going ape."

I ran back through toward the bedrooms. I expected the woman to lunge out of a dark corner and bash the bottle over my head. I opened the door to

Heather's room and found my sister lying face down on her bed, sobbing. "Heather, get up. We're in trouble."

She groaned into her pillow. "Mom was drinking."

"That's the least of our problems." I glanced out expecting to see Duke dogging my trail to tell me more stories of old people porn. I didn't see him anywhere. I licked my lips and then whispered, "We need to go."

Heather raised her face off the bed and stared at me with her red rimmed eyes. "Are you teasing me? It's not funny."

"Keep it down, Heather. I don't know who's listening."

"You didn't come with us when we left," Heather choked between words and had to pause to swallow. "Mommy begged you and begged you, but you wouldn't."

"She left dad. That's not how family works." I felt like I was speaking Duke's words and I didn't like it.

"Are we going to leave him now?"

I thought I saw a shadow move up the hallway. I stared out into the house, waiting. Was it a woman with a bottle and a bloody eye or a dead uncle with stories and plans? I'd seen worse in the house – glimpses. I was afraid to look away knowing some monsters moved when attention was drawn away.

"Maggie." Heather demanded my attention.

I dragged my eyes away from the hallway leading into the den of dead things. "What?"

"Dad? Mom? Are we leaving him again?"

"I don't know where dad is. He's probably out

wandering," I said.

"He's upstairs."

"You don't know that," I said.

"He went upstairs and he didn't come back down yet. He's upstairs and I don't want to leave him behind again."

"A lot has happened without you knowing, believe me," I said. "He might have slipped out."

"He's upstairs," Heather stated the fact in a flat tone.

"I'll go get him," I said. "Then, we get ready to go."

"Where's mom?"

I felt tears threatening to sting my eyes. I didn't want to scare or upset her. I fought it all back down and said, "She's sleeping on the couch. We can get her after we get dad."

"Where's Ms. Goshen? She was talking to mom in the kitchen."

That was the name of the social worker. Heather had told me about getting taken from mom and returned to dad. I assumed that was the woman mom tried to choke to death before I clobbered her with a frying pan. That conversation had apparently not gone well.

"She left, I think. Stay here and be ready to go as soon as I come back down with dad."

Heather climbed off the bed and took a step toward the door. "I'm going with you."

"That's a bad idea, Heather. Just let me go and get him back."

"I don't want to split up again," she said. "I was afraid I would never see you or dad again last time."

"Okay, but you stay with me," I said. "If I say we need to run back downstairs, we run, whether we have dad with us or not."

"Okay."

I wasn't sure running would make any difference, if we found ourselves in a situation where we had to run, but I wanted to believe that it would matter. Either way, we held hands and we walked down the hallway together. I started to feel dizzy and realized I wasn't breathing. I took several deep breaths to try to catch up.

"What's wrong?" Heather asked.

"Nothing. Keep going and stay quiet."

I wanted to check on mom, but I was afraid Heather would come undone and we'd never get out of there.

We reached the stairs and I stared up. I lifted my foot to take the first step and saw Duke leaning on the wall over near the entrance to the kitchen. He was holding his cigar again and a fat glass, with lime colored drink in it, that he sipped with one pinky up. I wondered if Heather could see the objects floating there in the air.

Duke tilted his head at me and winked. "He's on the third floor, so you may want to give up on this little rescue mission you have planned, Captain. There's nothing but trouble up there. It's getting crowded and not all the guests are happy right now, if you catch what I'm tossing."

"We have to go to the third floor?" I asked.

"Okay," Heather said, still holding my hand. "Let's go."

"You should rethink this whole thing," he said.

"Let things settle down. Let the new arrivals get comfortable with their roles and the accommodations. You and your family will be able to live in quiet again. We always need a generation to carry on things, so your family will be left alone for a while like before. You can go back to how things used to be. We all can. You can grow old, marry some fine gentlemen, and raise families of your own. The house is big enough. You can go home again, Captain. Sometimes you have no other choice."

"No," I said.

"Why not?" Heather asked.

"Yes, why not?" Duke laughed and took another sip. "Fighting is a bad idea for the living. You are so fragile. The brain breaks up like sponge cake. Bones snap. Organs pop. Aneurisms bubble up in bad arteries. You are fooled into thinking you'll be fine because you mostly heal sometimes. Getting knocked out isn't like in the movies. A concussion changes who you are. Getting choked until you have a bleed in the brain. Crashing in a car and rattling the brain around. Depriving the cells of oxygen. Shooting up and frying the synapses over and over. That damages the mind by damaging the wiring. People don't realize that we carry our brokenness into the afterlife with us. If we get addled on Earth, we will be cloudy and confused in the forever that follows. People think God will make it all better in the sugary sweet by and by. I believe in an afterlife, Captain, but I've never seen God and I haven't been able to rest yet."

"What's wrong?" Heather tugged at my hand in hers.

"Nothing," I said. "Let's go. Hurry."

Chapter 18
Foster Turner

I FELT SORRY for the little dead boy. He would drift into a wall and back out before apologizing. He would ask me where we were and what we were doing. I'd remind him about the woman in her underwear. He would remember with earnest, but then lose his focus again after a few steps. Eventually, he curled up in a corner and hugged his legs to his chest. I couldn't comfort him. I couldn't touch him. Long gashes erupted, dark and festering, along his arms and one side of his throat. He was settling in. I started to think he couldn't hear me anymore either.

That's when I heard the pounding on one of the doors. I watched it bounce in its frame a few down on the left. That was someone living. She was on the third floor with me, God help her.

I followed along the banister, looking down over the stairs to the second level. The wallpaper still clung to the walls there. The edge of the plastic showed where I never really intended to fix anything. These stairs were steeper than the others. Maybe the builder felt the spiritual severity as they were putting the place together. It was always meant to be a place that was haunted.

There was a brass key in the lock below the crystal knob. The room was locked with whoever was trying to get out. I squared myself in front of the door, holding onto the banister behind me. "Listen! I'm going to let you out. I can get you out of here, but you'll need to listen to me and we have to move quickly. Do you understand?"

The pounding paused and I waited for a response. The pounding resumed shaking the door and the wall around it.

I approached the door expecting to unleash some angry beast in the process. The key bobbed in the lock from the force of the impacts on the other side. I didn't outright remember the key. Not all the doors locked from the outside. I wasn't sure I wanted to know the histories of the ones that did. The swirl of brass at the end of the key's handle formed an elaborate triple leafed clover pattern. It rang a bell somewhere back in my head. I'm not sure where I had seen it before. If it was old enough, any of them could have used it to lock the room, but I had an idea who had done it. He had locked me in when he felt like I was bad.

I turned the key and felt the mechanism roll. The captive on the other side kept beating the door without trying the knob.

"Learned helplessness," I said.

I wrapped my hand around the crystal knob and turned. It actually turned slower with more resistance than the key had. It popped as the latch rolled free of the frame into the door.

The pounding stopped and I hesitated without pulling the door open. I wasn't ready for whatever new horror the house and the third floor had for me. The door erupted and struck me in the chin as it swung. I staggered back on my heels, wheeling my arms. The door had turned me punch drunk with one hook right to the button. I caught my balance for a second and waited to black out. It kind of surprised me when I didn't go down. I had started to think of myself as a guy that had a glass jaw.

I didn't recall what color her underwear used to be, but now it was brown and red with runners of blood. Her knuckles were busted open. She had cuts and scratches over her massive chest and sunken face. I couldn't remember how hurt she had been from Duke crashing the car. I wasn't sure if she was alive or not in that moment. Her eyes were wild and bloodshot themselves. They looked pinned like she was still high and her brain was about to cook itself in the chemicals. I had seen that a time or two back when I thought I was saving Ruthie.

Maybe I still could.

I only had the vaguest sense that she had to be alive to be hitting the door until she was bloody. If she died outside the house, she couldn't hit the door without touching it in life. Those were the rules as I understood them from Uncle Duke, assuming he was telling the truth, which was one hell of an assumption. All of this was only the hint of a thought that began to crystallize before she launched herself at me.

She screeched her curses at me without a break between syllables. "Cocksucker bastard piece of dog shit gonna tear out your mutherfucking eyes!"

I brought my hands up, but her claws got through and bit into my face. One bony knee and one sharp elbow drove into me and we went back into the banister. The wood splintered and folded back over the drop above the stairs.

I twisted and tried to keep from tumbling into space, but in the process, I dropped my hands and wasn't defending myself. She was closed fist striking my ribs and jaw with insane strength. I was spinning as I tried to get off the failing banister back to the warped boards of the floor. Her knuckles felt sticky as they pulled away from my shirt and skin from each punch.

I scrambled around, away from the edge. I had an opening to get away from her, but my knee twisted and locked on me. I fell to my knees and one hand. The pain raced up my back and I couldn't find my feet again.

Movement in the open room drew my attention. There was a broken chair in the center of the room and the old curtains that looked like someone threw up mustard. I saw his back. He was still wearing the sweatshirt from my high school football team and the green corduroy pants. He had his back to me so that I was staring at his bald spot instead of his face. I did not want to be on the third floor. I had no time for this. He yanked at one of the mustard colored drapes.

She lifted her fists above her head, as she stood over me. I turned my attention on her wild face in time to see her like some bloody priestess raising the blade for the sacrifice. Her weapon was a shank of wood, split to a rounded sharp edge. One side was the fresh white of the interior, hidden from the years of wear and stress. The outside was dark, the decay from exposure working from the outside in. I didn't know if the giant splinter was from the tilted banister or the shattered chair.

She brought it down and drove the point into my chest below the collarbone. All my strength and air melted out of me in an instant. It was replaced by an exquisite pain. The walls and edges went sketchbook black line again as the color left the world and took the sound with it. My eardrums put up a warning ring to let me know the sound had been stolen.

I remembered a snippet from a sports medicine class I had taken in college long after my dreams of playing were dashed and before I had resigned myself to choosing a real career in real estate. There is a bundle of nerves centered under the shoulder and collarbone and above the pectoral. It's a junction point for messages along the entire trunk of the body, including signals of pain and distress. The professor had tried to hold the class's attention by saying it was a favorite spot for torture because it maximized pain away from damaging an organ. I knew that spot exactly the moment she stabbed me. Then, she twisted the splinter, still stabbed inside me, and my nerves were on fire.

She wrenched the shaft out and a small spout of blood belched out with it. She came down again and stabbed me closer to the center of my chest. I felt the stick grind against bone, going in and coming back out. Some of the wood broke loose and stayed in as she pulled the weapon away. With all my will, I brought my arms up to defend myself. The point of her shank was broken into blunt fingers of blood soaked wood. As her next stab caught my forearm, I thought maybe it hurt more having the dull wood driven in than when it was still sharp.

My father charged out of the room into the hall then. He contacted the chair pieces and scattered them out into the hall ahead of him. He wrapped the curtain around her neck from behind and pulled her backward.

I saw his face again as I lay on my back, with the shaft of wood still sticking out of the meaty side of my right forearm. She clawed at the cloth wrapped around her neck and reached behind her head, but could not find the flesh of an enemy to grab. My dad's face and neck were sliced open in stripes. The flesh drooped and hung open to darkness, bone, and tendon underneath. The stump of his tongue was swollen and black in the back of his mouth forcing his teeth to hang open an inch or so.

He yanked her backward into the room, as she cried and screamed, "No. No. No."

She caught the leading edge of the door and slammed it closed as she was dragged back inside. Uncle Duke smiled at me from where he had been standing behind the door. He leaned out and twisted the key locking the door again. "Snoopy little brats don't get presents at Christmas, Foster."

I tried to get up, but coughed blood out onto my chin and fell back to my side.

Uncle Duke took my silence as an invitation to keep talking. "We used to have the pre dinner drinks up here, kid. The furniture was moved out onto the sundeck in the back and covered. Mother had the servants brown the chicken and she finished off with the sauce. We came back up here for after dinner drinks while the tables were removed and the furniture returned. When our tipsy guests would leave, they would find the downstairs all changed and sometimes come back up here saying they couldn't find the front door. We would laugh and laugh. We should start having dinner parties again, Foster. Do you think your wife could learn to make a good brown sauce?"

"Daddy!"

I rolled up to look down the hallway. Both the girls, Maggie and Heather, were standing at the end of the broken banister holding hands. I thought it was Maggie that had called to me, but Heather was the one that still called me daddy.

Uncle Duke said, "Mother could probably teach her if we could get both women focused long enough."

"No." My voice lost its wind at the end of my words. "Get out of here. Go to your mother and get out."

Maybe I was still able to save Ruthie and the girls too, if I didn't try to hold on so tightly.

"I'm disappointed in you, Foster," Uncle Duke said.

Maggie and Heather ran toward me. One of the doors burst open and a dresser with an attached mirror slid across, smashing through the last of the banister and dumping the broken railing onto the stairs below. Maggie pulled Heather back and around the side of the dresser. They were still coming. I tried to catch my breath to tell them to run away. They had stopped listening to me a long time ago though.

The woman in her locked room started beating again. She wasn't hitting the door though. It sounded like the window.

The dresser lifted off the lip of the broken railing posts. I could see the hands and arms, but not much more of the bodies. The dresser raced back and caught both girls. They stumbled and screamed. They tried to get away, but it shoved them back into the room with it and the door slammed closed.

I tried to get up, but collapsed to my stomach this time. I pulled at the wood in my forearm. Painful weakness stopped my efforts.

Uncle Duke took the key from the door with the bloody woman. He walked over and inserted it to lock Maggie and Heather inside their room.

"Stop," I breathed.

Uncle Duke turned to face me with his hands on his hips. He opened his mouth, but then clutched his skull with both hands. He groaned and said, "God, what is she doing now?"

He dropped down through the floor and was gone. It took all my energy to get up to my knees. Duke rose back up through the floor and yanked the key out of the lock. He walked around to the stairs and stepped down slowly. "Almost made a mistake there, didn't I, kid? I have too many irons in the fire because of you and that woman."

Chapter 19
Ruthie Turner

I RUSHED BACK into the house and it sounded like something destructive was going on upstairs, the house echoing with things breaking. Duke was gone, which didn't surprise me. I was glad for the respite.

The first level was empty. I could feel it. Everything was now focused on the third floor and I knew my family's lives depended on me. There was no hyperbole in the thought.

In the kitchen, I pulled two knives from the dishwasher, the two biggest I could find, and was ashamed to admit my eyes searched for the bottle of whiskey. When I didn't see it, I ran through the hallway before I took up more time looking for it while my children died upstairs. I wasn't going to let drugs and alcohol turn me back into the sniveling coward I'd been in my younger days.

I got to the first step leading up and hesitated, my foot hanging in midair like I was frozen. I didn't want to start on this path of no return. It felt like, if I went up, I was never coming back down.

Yet, if I didn't go and save my family, they'd be trapped upstairs with the ghosts of this house forever. I knew beyond a shadow of a doubt I might need to trade my life for Heather and Maggie's and I was suddenly fine with it. I was calm. I was their mother and I wouldn't forget it.

I took a deep breath and whispered, "Focus on the task at hand and be the perfect role model for them as they live a long and wonderful life."

"You missed your mark as a poet," Duke said from the top of the stairs. "What a shame. Imagine all the time wasted shooting junk into your veins and being promiscuous when you could've written out your pain instead of trying to medicate it. I told Foster from the beginning what a mess you'd end up being, but he was in love. The kid never listened to what was good for him and now he'll have to pay the price."

I gripped both knives in my hands and took the first step, staring at Duke with what I hoped was anger and not fear.

Duke sighed. He was missing his cigar, but patted down his pockets and smiled when he found it, pulling it out. He produced an ornate lighter and lit it, a ghostly blue light sparking from the lighter. I couldn't remember if I'd actually seen him smoking the cigar or if it had been for show.

"I guess we're going to settle all of this today, is that it, chicken? Someday in the far future, when we're all still the same age and haven't aged a second, we'll sit around as a group and tell funny stories about how this night went. We'll laugh and make fun of you for trying something so futile and insignificant. It will be a hoot, as the birth mothers and baby daddies say," Duke said. He waved his hand and took a step back above me. "Come on up, Ruthie. Everyone is waiting for you. I guess it would be cheating to go on with the show without you as the star. Isn't that what you've always wanted? To be the center of attention? To have a mommy and a daddy who doted on you when you were a kid? Didn't little Ruthie just want a hug?"

Whether he was doing it on purpose or not, his hateful stinging words were giving me strength. I took the steps at a quicker pace and halfway up my anger was boiling over and I was mumbling under my breath, hoping I could kill Uncle Duke just one more time.

I could smell the cigar smoke and it took me back to old, faded memories that became sharper as my mind reeled.

I'd been in a crack house as a teen and had been in a fevered dream, dancing on the razor's edge of overdosing and ending my pitiful life. I knew it was one of those days you can count on your hand when you had a fifty-fifty chance of living or dying.

I remembered the cigar smoke and the shadowy man who'd carried me out of the building and into the waiting arms of police officers. Had there been a fire?

I stopped walking and looked up at a smiling Duke, who blew smoke down the stairs in my direction.

"It was you who saved me from the crack house and got me help before I overdosed," I said.

"I was just doing what I had to for the family. Nothing personal. There are things in this and other worlds you cannot begin to fathom. Everyone acts like when they come to a fork in their road, they have a choice. What a sad little lie that is, I'm afraid. Everything is preordained and fits nicely into the box.

There are no real wild cards in this hand, Ruthie. We all have our role. I've known mine for a long time, even when I walked among the living. I always knew what I was going to do to get to this spot. This point in time. I also know what needs to be done from this moment on, and it isn't too pretty for you," Duke said.

"You talk too much," I said and started going up the stairs again. I didn't know if I could actually touch the man or if he could touch me, but I wanted to find out. More importantly, I wanted to know if the blades could touch his inhuman flesh or if they'd pass right through him to the wall behind.

Duke shrugged and took a step back as I got to the top of the stairs.

"Where is my family?" I demanded.

Duke threw his hands in the air. "All around us. Every last member of the Turner family will be joining us shortly, as well as some special guests from over the years. Friends and family, you might say. This is going to be one big party."

For every step I took forward, IDuke paced backwards, his eyes upon me. He didn't look scared or in control. He looked... like this was the way it was supposed to be. The plastic hanging from the walls billowed out and crinkled as it floated back down. I wondered if it was Duke providing the wind.

I stopped and I could see his passing look of alarm before he stopped, too.

"I thought you wanted to test those knives out," Duke said. "I'm wondering if the sheer anger you have for the Turner name is enough to solidify that emotion. I wonder if you can finally reverse the curse, as the catchy saying goes, and stop all this madness before it jumps to the next generation," Duke said.

I saw something in his eyes. Something... as if he was pushing me to do what needed to be done and secretly rooting for me to do it. Did he want out of this house as well? Did he want me to actually help him to finally rest in peace?

Duke slid to his right suddenly and went into an open door. I followed, knives at the ready to test my theory.

Duke was on the other side of the barren room, leaning against the window and looking outside.

"You know how long it took to dig up the graves and get every last piece of every last family member upstairs? That wasn't easy, especially when a nosy neighbor who couldn't sleep in the middle of the night glanced out the window. A restless husband sneaking to look at porn while the wife was asleep. A teenager sneaking back in after curfew. A random police car cruising by. A burglar in the bushes. Too many things to get in the way," Duke said.

I grinned. "I thought you said it was all preordained? Isn't that the big word you used? If this was all supposed to happen a certain way, you wouldn't have worried about someone seeing the horrible things you were doing."

Duke took the cigar out of his mouth and pointed it at me. "You're too smart for your own good, Ruthie. You really are a Turner, if only in name."

I approached him cautiously, as if he was a wounded and cornered animal. I guess in a way he was. I had no clue how I would get him to tell me what I wanted to know: where were my daughters?

And husband.

Foster was a Turner in blood. He'd been brought into the family business at a young age, or had he? Maybe he was as clueless as I had been. I could look back at certain snapshots of our relationship and really see where he was innocent of knowing what would happen if we lived in this house.

Then I remembered how insistent he'd been since the beginning to not sell this giant, old house and buy a condo closer to both our jobs in a more convenient area of Atlanta. He'd given me the sob story about his parents death and how much the house would be perfect when we had children, and it was paid for and we could get so many benefits out of not having a mortgage, on and on.

I'd fallen for it because I wanted to be with Foster in the beginning. Even when things turned weird and the girls were born, I sadly thought having children would put focus to Foster and his idiosyncrasies. How many times had I heard about a woman being in a bad marriage and suddenly pregnant and thinking she was a sucker, especially when she espoused how everything would be so much better now. I'd done it twice, hadn't I?

"Your move, chicken. We have a lot to accomplish in a short time," Duke said, pulling me back to the present.

I lunged at him with both knives, hoping to catch him off-guard and kill him once and for all.

Both blades struck against the wall behind where he'd been standing a second ago, the one in my right hand snapping in two and slicing my palm.

I dropped both knives and turned, blood spraying

as I moved.

Duke was right behind me and jumped back when the blood came near.

I reached out instinctively to punch him in the face, but he drew back. I managed to slap the cigar out of his mouth and, as it fell towards the floor, I dove and caught it.

Duke looked like I'd shot him in the face as he backed out of the room quickly and pointed a finger at me.

"You'll be sorry you did that, Ruthie. You can't change the future," he yelled, losing all of his former coolness and disappearing into thin air.

I cradled the cigar of a ghost and didn't know what to do next.

Chapter 20
MeLinda Goshen

SO COLD.

I opened my eyes to see I wasn't alone in the room. Dozens of people, all dressed in queer clothing, were around me, but no one was looking in my direction.

I was on the floor, in the far corner, and tried to stand on unsteady legs. I felt like I'd finished a case of whiskey instead of a few shots. My sight was fuzzy around the edges and it felt like people were getting bigger and smaller each second. I definitely needed to cut back until I sobered up again.

As a child, I loved Alice In Wonderland. The cartoon, the book, all of it. I felt like I'd slipped into the rabbit hole myself and it wasn't as pleasant a feeling as I'd thought it would be.

The room was freezing despite the Atlanta heat I knew was outside. I wanted to get out of the pressing crowd, but when I started walking I ended up back in the corner and my head was spinning.

An older woman who looked vaguely familiar turned and smiled at me. "When did you get here, hun?"

"I don't know. Just now," I said.

The room grew quiet and everyone turned to look at me.

"What's your name?" she asked.

"Melinda Goshen."

She clucked her tongue and stopped smiling. "You're not even a Turner. You're in the wrong room, dear."

"I want to leave," I said. "I need to leave this house."

Everyone laughed and I felt embarrassed, my face getting hot. I started to run toward the door, but the room was so long and narrow. I felt like I was falling then, spiraling down the rabbit hole again while everyone laughed. Hundreds of unfriendly voices joined in unison.

I pushed through people, but it was as if they were crowding me on purpose, making this tougher than it needed to be.

"You can't leave this house unless a Turner lets you," someone said in my ear. When I turned around, it was all laughing faces and mean looks.

"I need to leave the room," I shouted.

The crowd parted and I could see the open doorway now. I headed toward it, expecting it to shrink away and tease so I'd never escape.

But I was through and into the hallway.

The door slammed behind me and I felt vulnerable and alone.

This hallway was the last place I wanted to be. I just knew it and I spun on my heels, looking for an escape.

I fought against the nearest door. I had to get out of the hallway. It wasn't safe. I could feel the pressure of eyes upon me like I was underwater and dropping like a stone into the deep without proper gear. My lungs were going to be crushed and the pressure in my skull would push my eyes out.

The handle wouldn't turn no matter how hard I tried. I was panicking now and felt a definite presence coming at me from the far end of the darkened hallway.

I turned my head both ways. Pitch black evil emanated from both ends and I realized the stairs to the next level down were now gone, just a flat wall with crumbling wallpaper where I'd likely come up. Just a hallway and many doors.

The darkness moved like tar, inches at a time in my direction. Both ends of the hall.

I threw myself against the door, hoping to bust it in and then perhaps climb out a window. I'd rather jump to my death than be eaten alive by oily evil.

I was standing in a room, empty except for the two Turner girls.

The youngest turned and looked in my direction.

"Heather, right?" I asked.

She didn't answer, turning back to the window she'd been looking out.

I stepped forward and sighed. I felt so tired. I knew with all of the odd shit going on in the house the girl being rude and ignoring me was the least of my problems, but it still ticked me off.

"Excuse me, Heather, but I was trying to talk to you," I said.

She didn't turn to look at me, but her sister did.

"Your sister is so rude," I said. I could see trees outside. I was likely on the third floor of this massive house. No way I'd be able to climb down without losing my nerve.

"I'm Maggie. I know who you are," Maggie said.

Heather turned and looked at her sister.

"Who are you talking to?" Heather asked.

Maggie pointed at me. "Miss Goshen is in the room with us."

Heather looked confused and moved her head slowly from side to side like I was invisible.

"That's not funny," I said.

"Heather can't see you," Maggie said to me and crossed her arms with a frown. "You're part of the house now."

"I don't understand," I said. I was cold and tired.

"You're dead."

Chapter 21
Foster Turner

I DRAGGED MYSELF up to my feet and regretted it as I leaned against the wall between the doors to the woman's room and the one to where the girls were held. As I bled down the boards marring the wallpaper strips that still clung to the third floor walls, I heard wood splintering in that woman's room. She couldn't break the glass for some reason, but, by the sound of it, she seemed to be trying to claw her way through the walls. If she did, she might end up in the room with the girls.

I closed my hand on the locked knob to the girls' door. I pulled and twisted, but it would not give. I felt the crushing pain of the effort in my bloody chest. I felt the pull of the shaft of wood still embedded in my arm.

I tried to call out to them, but I couldn't draw the air.

I lifted my foot as I leaned on the wall and kicked down on the knob. The entire world spun. I knew I was going to fall, but I kicked again and again. The pain in my knee and back were swallowed by the wounds in my chest.

The knob snapped off and bounced across the

floor and over the edge where the railing had been. I heard it continue to thump down the stairs alerting the house and everything in it to my vandalism.

I tried to reach for the door, but went down to my knees. The knob had broken along a weak point in the brass shaft and had snapped loose in a curved sharp edge that reminded me of the broken piece that woman had used to stab me.

I ran my fingers along the edge of the door and left bloody trails where I touched.

I took a deep breath and felt wet pain in my lungs. I gagged on what felt like something caught in my throat; I couldn't swallow. The heave of my chest hurt to the point I thought I was going to pass out. I'm going to die here, I thought. I was always going to die here.

I took one gurgling breath and growled out. "Maggie ... Heather ..."

I wasn't sure if it was blood or spit flicking out on my chin.

Someone started beating on the inside of the door, causing it to bounce in the frame, but the lock held. The old lock was separate from the knob. It held.

Maggie shouted from the other side. "Daddy, we can't get out."

I turned my head to look up the hallway, away from the stairs. I wanted to flee down the stairs, but I thought the way out might be deeper in the house. Some things needed to be faced. I had to catch my breath between sentences and never quite could. "I'm going to get help. I'll come back. If your mother finds you first ... leave with her. Don't come back."

"We're not leaving you," Heather said.

"If you get out before I get back," I said as I clutched my chest, "get out of the house with your mother. We have to be apart for a while to save the family."

"Promise you'll come back," Heather yelled.

I opened my mouth, but I didn't say anything. I turned my face back up the hallway again. I felt myself start to slide and I was worried if I hit the floor, I wouldn't be getting back up again. I forced myself up to my feet and worked my way around until I was back in the narrow hallway with the rotten ceiling leading back toward the room.

I didn't see the boy again. Maybe he was folded into the fabric of the house with the rest of them.

I tried to stay in the middle as I lifted my feet one after the other moving down the hall to where I had to go, but never wanted to. I stumbled to the left and braced one hand on the wall to catch myself. The wood was spongy and the top surface felt like it wanted to slide off under the pressure of my off balance weight. I took a couple more steps and leaned too far to the right. I caught myself on the edge of a doorframe and my thumb crumbled away part of the wet wood.

I thought I might pass out and part of me wanted to. I wanted to die, but not in there.

I finally caught hold of the knob for the room at the end. It was all brass and cold. I thought that in the way knobs got hot because there was fire on the other side, maybe this one was so cold because of what lay behind it.

I turned it hoping it would be locked – that I would have an excuse to fail. It turned and swung in on darkness. Unlike the blackness that held deep to the edges and corners of this house, this darkness was shifting and flowing like a living thing. There was nothing living in the room though except me as I stepped through and I wasn't positive about myself. The pain of trying to breathe was my only clue I might still be alive, but I thought from what I had seen in the house, death might hurt too.

My eyes adjusted to the odd light. I looked up and realized I was looking at the sky through blistered rafters of the broken roof. Crumbled shingles bit into my bare feet and I was sure I was going to find a nail this time. The floor was sticky. My first impression was that a fire had blackened all the wood above me. Then, I felt the water drip on my forehead and shoulder.

I lowered my eyes and it all changed the way I knew it would. The walls were painted with blood. It was fresh and thick, running down and dripping with chunks of hair and gristle mixed into the splatter. If someone had orchestrated it for a movie, I'd accuse them of being over the top, but I knew this was all a real reflection of what had happened – an echo – because I had seen it after my father hacked away at my mother. Maybe even then I was seeing blood from past murders and slaughters. Maybe the scenes of gore were a magnet for the psychic violence that had powered and poisoned this house for generations.

I remembered Duke locking me in the room for hours and overnight when I was bad.

I looked up again at the sky and wished I could fly free without dying and becoming one of them. "Remember back when the house used to have a roof?"

I felt my head throb and spin and I started to think my blood pressure was dropping.

When I looked down again, the walls were dark and spotted with mold. I knew the blood had been cleaned. Uncle Duke had been there when we did it. There had been old wooden scrub brushes with coarse yellow bristles. It hadn't been long before they were caked with gore and I was just pushing the blood around more that cleaning it up. Buckets and mops sloshed through it. We poured water through the mop heads until we clogged the sinks and washed bloody puddles into the yard after that. I was numb to it by the time we were done.

Along the floor, discolored clothes were wrapped in bundles that lined the back wall of the decaying room. I couldn't tell if the clothes had been towels, sheets, canvas, or something else. These were Christmas presents of the damned. Brown and black bone poked through the corners. Other bodies lay more intact in shrouds that maintained a more human shape. Hair lay out on the floor from a break in one shroud. It was caked with what could have been mud or feces.

Melinda Goshen's body was cast aside on top of the heaps of bundled bones. Her neck was twisted back and bulging in two spots. Her eyes stared up with glassy reflections of the sky above like she was hoping for the same escape I was. Her clothes provided a shock of color over everything else that took on the drab tones of earth and rot. She did not look like a person sleeping. Her body was already sunken and emptied out from death.

Everything I touched was drawn into death including this woman who was trying to keep my girls safe, but just brought them back here to die too. I could not remember if I had been the one that had done it to her. Duke had made me into a killer. Had he brought all these bodies up here or had I? Did Duke carry Goshen up here? I thought he could only touch stuff he had contacted in life, but I couldn't imagine her climbing up here alone with her throat crushed or her neck twisted. He had driven the car too when he crashed it. Maybe he was able to do more than I thought.

I turned to the bed and my mother sat in the sunken, black center of the mattress. Blood pooled around her and covered most of the tears in her clothes and skin that showed white bone underneath. Her bones had maintained better than the bundles.

She smiled, spreading open her throat with the exposed cords pulling taut. Her smile lit up the room for a moment. The paper on the walls was suddenly bright. Fresh flowers sat on the side tables. Then, we were back to darkness and neglect.

She said, "I do remember when there was a roof."

Even death could not kill the softness of her voice. I leaned on the foot of the bed trying to keep my balance. I was seeing a puffy, white comforter splattered with her blood, but I was feeling a gritty, bare mattress under my hand. I wasn't sure what was real in this room, including myself.

"I'm in trouble, mom. I can't stay here."

"You are always welcome here," she said. "You should visit more often."

I closed my eyes in a long blink. I wasn't sure I

could get her to understand. Not in here. This was a bad idea.

"The house is dangerous, mom. This room … is full of bodies. The spirits are dangerous and they are trying to hurt my wife and my girls."

"I can't wait to meet them."

I couldn't look at her smile. As much as I was drawn to it, the gaping holes in her throat and chest were too much. It was like having her die all over again. I blinked and looked toward the door to the room. It was still open, but it looked like it had swung farther closed. I was worried the longer I stayed the more that gap would tighten until there was no way out. I would go through the door and find myself back in this room with her, and the bodies, and the blood that someone needed to clean up even after the sinks were clogged.

I had been bad and Uncle Duke would need to teach me another lesson with another locked door.

"I want them to be free of this place," I said. "The others don't want to come in here. You have some sort of power that they don't. I need to know how to cut my wife and children loose from this place, mom. Can I trade myself to let them go? I'll do anything."

"I don't know if that will work," she said. "You can't get away from family. Lots of Turner men have tried to cut their way out of their problems in their time, Lord knows. You can't really run from your past, Foster. After all, you are still here and back in this room. You can throw yourself on the grinder and we all do eventually. You can try to cut the people you love to try to set them free, but I don't think it will make any difference for your girls, son."

"Is there no way you can give me permission to set them free? Please, mother."

My stomach hurt and I bowed my head. I couldn't remember the last time I had eaten, but my bowels felt watery like I was about to have an accident. For all my contact with death, I had never actually died to know what it was like, but that's what I thought of as these feelings came on and weakness spread deep through my muscles.

"Disowning family is a terrible thing. It may not be worth it, Foster. You don't want to be alone in this life or the one to come. Being without family is terrible."

"I need to disown the family?" I asked. "Is that the key?"

"You can't change who you are?"

I stared down at the mattress watching it shift from bare and empty to full and bloody as my vision focused in and out.

"Then, I need to disown them?"

I heard my mother sigh, but it sounded like air escaping her torn throat. She said, "That would be a terrible thing, but I believe in you. I know you will do the right thing."

"Is that the right thing, mother? Is that how it will work?"

"I need to rest." Her edges grew fuzzy and she appeared to be sinking into the blood. The pool rose and spilled over the edges around the folds of the comforter. Blood oozed onto the floor in several spots as she submerged and then the blood soaked through the wide gaps in the floor. I tried to picture what was below this room on the second floor, but I couldn't mentally pull up the geography of the house.

I pushed myself up to my feet and hobbled over broken shingles. I tracked blood through the doorway and back into the hallway. I couldn't find the walls with my hands as I teetered in open space. I looked down at my bloody footprints thinking it was my mother's blood, but then realizing I had torn my own feet and was stepping through the blood still falling from my chest and soaked shirt.

I went to my knees so suddenly that I thought the house and hallway had moved. I tried to get back to my feet, but my knee buckled and I fell sideways into one of the doors. It splintered and I found myself in a room of rolled, stacked carpets. There were covered paintings in loose canvas leaning against the wall. The room smelled like the swamps where I used to hunt with my father. Holes in the ceiling opened to the darkness of the attic above.

I turned back toward the door, but the motion made me feel dizzy. I then fell forward and only just got my face turned before I bounced the side of my head on the floor. I was shivering uncontrollably and tried to remember if that was a symptom of shock.

I saw his shoes as he paced up the hallway, toward me, to the open doorway. I tried to scoot back away from him, deeper into the room, but did not make it far. As I spoke from my belly on the warped floor next to the soaked carpets, the noises didn't sound like words in my ears anymore. "I'm letting them go. They are not my girls anymore. They are Ruthie's and she is not mine anymore, either. I forgive her for wanting to go and I set them all free to go their own way. Now, you can take me, but you can't have them."

He stepped into the room and stopped by my head, kneeling down. I lifted my eyes and felt them jumping back and forth in my sockets like I was trying to go into REM sleep. It wasn't Duke. My dad was staring down at me with the black hunk of death in his mouth where the stump of his tongue kept him from closing his teeth.

He laid his hand on my back and I felt his fingers cold against my shoulder blade. It felt good.

I saw her pass the doorway in a hurry. I thought it was Ruthie. Was she looking for me? I tried to listen, but all I heard was a roar in my ears that was like a rushing river.

"I need to get off the fucking floor," I said.

He took hold of my shoulders in both his hands.

Chapter 22
Ruthie Turner

IF THE CIGAR was a blunt laced with marijuana, I'd be taking big pulls from it to get my nerves in check and my thoughts focused.

Instead, I blew on the tip to make sure there was still the hint of heat. I was beginning to put it all together and I needed to use the cigar to get it done.

I was in the hallway of the third floor. The rest of the house didn't matter. It never mattered. This is where all of it started from and ended . This single hallway and the dozen doors coming off of it. We'd just assumed the entire upper floors were bathed in blood, but it was just dripping through the rotten cracks in the floor and dropping on our scared heads.

I wasn't scared anymore.

If I had to die in this house, so be it. My only goal was saving my girls. I knew I was strong when it came to this, but afterward I'd need to fall off of a very tall wagon and bury my psyche in the hard stuff until I overdosed or was dragged to jail or rehab. My life was going to be sacrificed for Heather and Maggie.

I looked at the moldy ceiling and sighed. Was there an actual God up there, surveying the scene with knowing eyes and watching it play out in silence? Would he bother to help us? Could he in such an evil place?

The cigar was going out so I took a shallow puff and watched the orange glow light up the hallway. My lungs burned and I thought about being trapped in the burning trailer again.

"You're playing a dangerous game," Duke said from the other end of the hallway. He looked odd without his cigar prop and his face looked older, more haggard, in the thin lighting. I realized there was a hole in the ceiling about halfway between us, jaundice light yellowing the warped and wet wood.

"I'll make you a deal, Uncle Duke: let me, Heather and Maggie walk out of the house untouched and I won't ever look back. You can live here with my soon to be ex-husband and do whatever crazy things you Turner nuts do in your spare time. I'm going to live out the rest of my days far away from this street, this city, this state... I think California is the place to be."

I could see his face turn to anger but tinged with fear. "You know I can't let you go, chicken."

I snorted, "You mean you can't let the girls go. You could care less about me."

He looked hurt and shook his head. "We can't do this without you, Ruthie. If I could let anyone go, I would. I promise. You think I like doing this? I want to be gone from this house myself." Duke glanced up, but I didn't know if he was thinking about a higher power or wondering if the ceiling was going to cave in on us if I was successful.

"I'm going to get my girls and leave," I said.

Duke looked back at me and shook his head. "What about your husband?"

The thinnest smile flittered across his lips before it was gone. Duke was testing me.

"I'll trade Foster for my girls. Shit, I'll trade my soul for the safety of Heather and Maggie," I said. I pushed my chest out and pointed a finger at Duke, but also took into account the many ghosts listening to our conversation, the house holding its breath. "Step off to the side and let me get to my family. Understand?'

Duke did the unexpected and shuffled to his right, away from the nearest door. He shrugged his shoulders.

"What are you doing?" I asked.

"I can't harm you physically. I thought you knew that. All I can do is manipulate you to do things you want to do anyway. Have I ever touched you? No. I can't. I'm not alive, Ruthie, just a revenant trapped inside this house. I'm just trying to appease the rest of the family. I do it all for the Turner name, you have to believe me," Duke said and put his hands up. "But you need to get out before it's too late."

Was it a trick? My mind was still foggy from everything that had happened. I needed to concentrate and get my girls out of this madhouse. I thought I remembered him carrying me.

I took two quick steps, expecting Duke to flinch and attack, but he actually leaned against the wall and looked bored, his hands still in the air.

"Any chance, once you're ready to leave, I get my cigar back? I've really grown fond of the taste after all these years. It's become a part of me," Duke said.

"I'll think about it," I lied. I had no intention of doing anything remotely nice to a guy who caused my family so much trouble and pain over the years.

It dawned on me he'd always been a part of our lives. Every move Foster had made was because of the Turner family. I could think of a dozen times over the years he'd changed his mind suddenly and without a satisfying answer about something we'd planned.

We never went on long trips, the girls weren't allowed to do too many sleepovers at a friend's house and never had friends over. Not that the girls would want anyone to see where they lived. The neighbors had once remarked we lived at 1313 Mockingbird Lane and I had to agree. It was a big, foreboding structure to the onlooker. It was infinitely more horrible from the inside.

Duke moved his wrists closer and tapped on an imaginary watch. "Time's wasting, chicken. You need to hurry before the rest of the family figures out your game plan."

I was scared.

What if I opened the door to an empty room... or worse?

"Heather and Maggie better be alright," I said to Duke as I walked toward the room, trying to look brave. I needed to be strong in the face of this unknown.

Foster and I had watched a movie once where the guy opened up a box and saw, presumably, the head of his dear wife inside. He lost his mind and began shooting the killer. Foster and I had an argument afterwards. He said the guy should've been calm and let the law handle what had happened and grieved about his lost spouse. I told him I would've shot the guy until the gun ran out and taken my partner's as well.

What would I do if my girls were now part of the peeling wallpaper, trapped inside this house? Would I freely join them to keep the family together?

I put my hand on the doorknob and looked at Duke.

"If this is a trick, you'll wish you'd never been born," I said.

Duke shrugged. "I wish that every day, Ruthie. Yet... there are some things you can't change in this life or in the afterlife."

I turned the doorknob and pushed open the door, ready to face whatever it was I needed to face.

"You dumb bitch," Xandra, wearing bra and panties, shrieked as the door swung open. She charged me.

Duke grabbed me by the shoulder and spun me around, his fingers digging into my skin. His grip was real.

"Get the cigar before she burns the place down, chicken, and I'll let you walk out of here alive," Duke yelled.

Chapter 23
Xandra

I HOPED THE strange guy wasn't bullshitting me. Right then I had no time to stop and ask as he tried to drive Ruthie down and against the door.

If he wasn't blocking me in the room, my goal would be to run past and down the steps, but he was too big and Ruthie was struggling too much.

I saw the cigar in her hand and swiped to knock it out of her grip.

"Don't let the cigar hit the wood," the guy yelled. "She'll burn the damn house down. Pin her arms."

I grabbed Ruthie by the arm holding the cigar, but she sucker punched me in the face and I felt my nose break. The pain was excruciating. I hadn't had it broken in years and now I was pissed.

An old boyfriend once said I thrived in chaos. In a situation that was out of hand, I could rise to the occasion and throw a few haymakers and get away. It was a gift.

This was absolute chaos as the guy tried to swing Ruthie against the wall, propelling everyone into the room I'd been trapped in. The momentum pitched her to the ground where she skidded across the bare floor. I could hear the dry wooden floor creaking and cracking until she stopped.

The guy looked at me and smiled.

"Thanks, chicken. As soon as we choke the life out of her, we can get you back to the crack house or trailer park you crawled out from under. Deal?"

"Fuck you," I said, but thought better of fighting him. If he wanted to think I was just some crack whore, let him think it. I was better than that.

I tried to put my nose back into place, but I saw stars instead. The intense pain got my head spinning and I felt myself falling to the floor.

My head felt like it was going to explode and a white sheet of pain flashed before my eyes. I couldn't see, gripping the sides of my head and wanting to squeeze it until it popped and I was done with this.

It was all too much chaos, even for me.

I stumbled to my feet and shook the stars from my sight.

The guy was on one knee, next to Ruthie, both hands around her throat. Her face was drained and I knew she'd be dead in a few minutes, if he didn't stop.

I didn't care. I owed the bitch nothing, and all I wanted was to get out. I turned to see the open door and ran for it.

He was quicker than I thought, jumping back at me as I passed him. His hand snaked out and grabbed my ankle, and I went forward and slammed against the wall inches from the door and freedom.

I fell onto my back and saw the drywall had been ripped in two from the force of me going in head-first. The pipes were exposed, ancient and rusty.

"You're not leaving until she's dead. We have a

deal," he said.

"He's lying. Xandra. He's going to kill you next," Ruthie said as she struggled to stand, falling back on her ass before finally scuttling against the wall.

"I don't care about either of you. I only care about myself," I said. This wasn't my fight. I didn't care who won or lost, just who could help me escape.

Ruthie stood and held the cigar in front of her face.

"I'm going to burn this house down unless you tell me where my girls are," Ruthie said. She blew on the end and it glowed brightly. "I'll count to three."

I sidestepped a few inches closer to the door. He glanced at me before turning slightly, keeping both me and Ruthie in his sight now.

"Your girls are safe, but they won't be for long unless you put the cigar down. You haven't had enough fire in your life lately?" the guy said as he inched closer to Ruthie. As soon as I took a step forward, he retreated, filling the doorway with his bulk. I wasn't going to get out this way, but the windows hadn't budged; it was like they were bulletproof. I'd peeled away wood from one of the walls until my fingers were bloody, but got nowhere.

I turned, frantically searching for another exit. Maybe there was a door to another room? No. Not even what might be a closet door. This room was solid... or was it?

I looked at the space near the door where I'd caved in the drywall. The pipes probably ran up from the kitchen or maybe a bathroom underneath. Water pipes in these old houses were frail and rusting and I could bust them and get into the hallway before this guy knew what I'd done, but I needed a major distraction from Ruthie.

I played possum and took a few steps into the corner, faking a crying fit so he'd think of me as a weak woman and worry about the one threatening to burn the house down.

Ruthie decided I was her distraction and she stood, running to the window and driving her elbow into it. The window didn't break. I'd been trying that move for hours without success.

He wasn't taking the bait and trying to stop her though; he still had on me.

"I'm trying to save you, Ruthie. Your girls need you. This family needs you. We can make this work, you know? Stop fighting it. Foster's parents would love to meet you," he said.

Ruthie turned and now she looked pissed. Any semblance of fear or confusion had left her face. A second ago she'd looked tired and resigned to the fact we were all going to die, but now she looked energized by his words.

"I'm done talking, Duke. I'm done with you, this house, Foster, and especially his dead parents who've ruled my life from the shadows for too long." Ruthie blew on the cigar end again. "Are they here, on the third floor? A pile of bones in a box or an urn? Scattered into the framework of the house? They will be once I'm done. I'd rather kill us all then take a knee to another Turner."

Ruthie dropped to one knee and placed the cigar near the floor and a cracked gap in the wood.

The guy closed his eyes for a second and sighed.

"You don't know what you're doing. You'll ruin

everything," he said but didn't try to stop her. He also didn't move away from the door and let me go.

The dry and ancient wood sparked for a second and then Ruthie jumped back in obvious surprise as the wood caught fire and began to smoke, an angry flame shooting across the floor like it was covered in gasoline.

I had seconds before the room was engulfed and we all died. This bitch was determined to see me burn.

I turned and kicked, with all my might, against the pipes.

"You burned down my trailer and tried to kill me. Your family has been trying to use fire against me all this time. Guess what, Uncle Duke? I'm going to burn the Turner home to the ground. Nothing but rubble. They'll pave this lot over for a new house," Ruthie said.

The fire licked up both sides of the wall, spreading in all directions.

I threw a shoulder against the pipes, hoping I could dislodge one and squeeze between them. The drywall on the other side had come undone and I could see the hallway and freedom, but the pipes were too tight to squeeze through.

He was still in the doorway, looking sad and unmoving.

I kicked again and the pipe came loose with an awful tearing noise. The pipes to either side made a gurgling popping noise and I was covered in dirt and water as the ceiling above me began to collapse.

Something screamed above me, and I saw the rest of the ceiling was buckling like a house of cards.

Water streamed from myriad cracks as the rainwater, collected for decades, finally found its way down and splashed into the room, a nauseating stench of dead leaves and dead things.

"No. This can't be happening," Ruthie yelled.

The fire was being extinguished faster than it could grow.

The house was coming down around me. I turned to the doorway but the guy was now gone. All that work and now I could step through the door.

But not before Ruthie ran at me and threw a punch, slamming into my broken nose again.

"You've ruined everything," Ruthie yelled. She pushed me to the ground and was out of the room, screaming her daughters' names.

A chunk of ceiling fell within inches of my head, shattering on the floor. There was still fire in the room and now smoke filled the space.

I crawled into the hallway, keeping low, and ignoring the angry sounds of a shifting house above me. If the rest of the ceiling caved in, I'd end up on the ground floor under a pile of rubble.

I found the stairs and took them three at a time, my body threatening to tumble and crack open my head. I ran down the steps past the second floor and didn't stop running until I was outside.

The steps were packed with people, all staring at me quietly as I blasted past them, out onto the front lawn and to the street without looking back. I ran into a tan Buick. I'm not sure what model it was. It was running and the keys were in it. I was never one to look a gift horse in the mouth. I climbed in and started driving without even closing the door. I made it out of the neighborhood and about a mile down the road still not knowing where I was when the blue lights came on behind me. I really hit the gas then.

Chapter 24
Ruthie Turner

THERE WAS A God and he was testing me like he'd been doing my entire life. I needed to believe the world wasn't just chaos and disorder. I needed His power to help me find my girls before the house collapsed around me.

The fire had been stopped, but Xandra had caused a chain reaction, pulling the house down around us. After all of this, to die crushed by a falling house beam so close to my girls would be heartbreaking.

"Maggie! Heather!"

I ran down the hallway, knowing they had to be up here somewhere. I banged on the first door when it didn't open.

The room I'd been in was screaming in protest and I could hear snapping wood. The house was going to come down around my head and my fear was I'd be killed, buried a few feet from my daughters without ever knowing it.

My bigger fear was being trapped in the house, as a ghost, with my daughters and the rest of the Turner family.

I began to pray as I got to the next door and tried it. Also locked. I pounded on the wooden frame, shouting for my daughters. Nothing. I passed an open door full of wet carpets. I kept shouting their names as I saw bloody footprints leading to one door at the end of the hall.

"Maggie? Heather?"

Something muffled answered me from the other side.

A kick jarred the door, but didn't open it, so I put all of my weight behind the kick and the door swung so fast and hard it slammed against the door and closed again.

In the split second I'd seen into the room, I knew my daughter's weren't inside, but there was someone I needed to face. Several people, in fact.

I opened the door and calmly walked in with a smile and the resolution that I'd speak my mind before continuing the quest for my daughters.

"Hello, Turner family. I finally get to meet you in the flesh," I said, pointing at the piles of bones in the room and laughing at my own joke. I wasn't going to show them anything but contempt and hatred.

When I saw Miss Goshen, her body broken on the pile, I looked away. There was no time to worry about her. She was gone. I wondered if I'd killed her or if the house had, and if it was really the same thing anyway.

"Hello, dear. Welcome to the family. I never got to officially welcome you," the old woman said, her features slightly distorted when I looked right at her. This was the matriarch of the Turner clan and Foster's mother who I'd only seen in a couple of hidden pictures.

The rest of the people in the room, perhaps a

dozen, shimmered in and out of view like holographic images. As if they were trying to stay in this world, even if only for a few seconds at a time. They huddled back in this room next to their bones as the rest of the house came apart in the wash.

His mother was the one I wanted to deal with, anyway.

"You're too late. I'm not part of this family and never was. I'll be putting in the papers to divorce your son as soon as I get my daughters and leave. We'll never come back and never think of the Turner family again. I'll be changing back to my maiden name and getting the court to change Heather and Maggie's last names as well. We'll move far away and you'll fade into memory like this house," I said.

I knew I was pushing her buttons and it wasn't wise, but the look on her face was worth it. She was angry and I'd struck a nerve.

I bent down and looked at the piles of bodies.

"Which one is yours, old hag? Ah, it must be this one. Still wearing the dress you died in that was out of style then. Still has enough fabric on it to make a nice pyre," I said. I'd been clutching the cigar and hoped it still had something left in it.

I blew on it, but there was only a very faint life to it and not enough to start anything.

I looked up and she was smiling.

"You can't win," she said simply.

Uncle Duke was standing next to her with his arms folded across his chest. He didn't look happy.

I stood and tossed him the cigar, which he caught, startled, and put it in his mouth.

"I've already won. I have no doubt I'll be safe and

able to escape with the only members of this family who matter," I said. I looked at Duke and nodded slightly. Either I'd made a fatal error and misjudged the man or I'd done the only thing I could do.

Uncle Duke pulled his lighter from his pocket and lit his cigar, puffing it until it was lit.

"You know I hate you smoking around me," she said without taking her eyes off of me. "It's a disgusting habit."

"I'd say I'll probably die from smoking, but... well, you know," Duke said. He closed the lighter and winked at me. "How'd you know where to come, chicken?"

"I didn't. I guessed. Where are my daughters?" I asked.

Duke pointed to his left. "Last door on this side around the corner. One with the missing knob. They're fine. I imagine they're ready to get out of this dump, too. I left a present in the door for you while the others weren't looking."

"Where's Foster?"

Duke shook his head. "You know the only way you leave is without him. I'd start doing what you need to do and then run like a gazelle. Also, might consider picking a name we don't know to look for, Ruthie Sullivan-Turner. We will be looking."

Foster's mother turned, hands on hips even though she was in the bloody bed, and stared daggers at Uncle Duke.

"What have you done?" She spit.

"What I should've done a long time ago. I'm sick of this house, truth be told. You were never much company when we were alive. I never understood what my nephew saw in you, chicken. You're not very nice," Duke said and tossed me his lighter.

She turned and watched the flight, reaching for it. Too late.

I caught it and dropped back down to the ground, opening the lighter and sparking the flame to the edge of her crumbling dress.

"The house might come down without that," Duke said.

"Better safe than sorry." The body was on fire and it spread to the many others in the room.

I stood and nodded at Duke.

He put out a hand. "I need my lighter for the afterlife. I'm sure there's smoking in Heaven. Definitely smoking where I'm likely going to, anyway."

I threw it without aiming and left the room as she started berating Uncle Duke, closing the door behind me. I didn't know where my husband was and I didn't need to look for him. He belonged with these people.

I belonged with my daughters, who I needed to find.

A hand grabbed for me out of one of the doorways, but I swatted it away and kept running. The house and the creatures in it were not going to hold me any longer. I didn't look back.

I rounded the corner to the end of the hallway and heard the floor collapse away behind me. I knocked on the door without a knob as more walls fell away, taking a large part of the house with it.

"Mom?" Heather asked from the other side.

Chapter 25
Maggie Turner

"MOM?" HEATHER YELLED again.

"There's no doorknob on the other side," Ms. Goshen said clutching her head. "The key is back in the lock though. I tried to turn it, but I couldn't."

"What's wrong with you?" I asked.

Ms. Goshen went to her knees and seemed to be coming apart like smoke being blown away. She said, "I feel like I'm dying."

I thought she might be making a joke, but then she was gone.

I heard the lock click and the door swung. Mom was on the other side. She looked like she had been beaten and she was soaking wet and dirty. Heather fell into her arms.

The floor cracked under me and tilted away at an angle. The wall behind me crumbled and fell into the gap left by the collapsing floor. Water sprayed out and washed down the wood taking pieces of it along with it.

"Maggie!" My mother reached for me. I ran to her, feeling the floor splitting under me.

She scooped Heather up in one arm and me in the other. She ran with one of us on each shoulder. It didn't feel real with boards falling from the ceiling and the floor opening up behind her as I watched. I thought I was too big for her to carry me anymore, but she was running with both of us. She was using a level of strength I only associated with my father.

Heather yelled, "We can't leave, Daddy. He said he was coming back. He promised."

"No, he didn't," I said.

"He did," Heather yelled. "He promised. I heard him."

He had been yelling to us through the door as he tried to kick it open. Heather asked him to promise to come back, but I hadn't heard him say anything. I thought Heather heard what she wanted to hear. I thought maybe we all did. As mom took us down the steep stairs in her arms, I felt so sorry that I had listened to Uncle Duke and participated in tricking her into coming back. At the same time, I felt good being in her arms, even with the house falling down around us and my mother's shoulder pushing into my sternum, making me feel like I was going to throw up.

As we went down the stairs, I saw him through the sprays of water and falling debris. I'm sure of it. Dad was between two men holding him up by his shoulders. One was Uncle Duke with a soggy cigar coming apart in his mouth. The man on dad's other side I didn't know. He was wearing a college sweatshirt, I think.

We went down below the level of the third floor and I didn't see him anymore. Mom slipped on broken wood and bounced on her butt on the steps. She tilted back as she fell to keep from dropping us. She regained her feet and ran out on the second floor.

Heather reached back over her shoulder at the stairs we had left. "Dad. Dad. Don't leave him."

Mom yelled, "He's already chosen to leave us."

Heather buried her face in mom's shoulder and bawled. I wanted to tell her that dad had tried to save us. He had told us to go with mom even if he couldn't get back to us. I wanted to argue that he loved us as much as she did, but she wasn't ready to hear it. With the house falling down on top of us, it wasn't a good time either.

Mom stumbled on something and almost fell again. A broken doorknob shot out from under her feet. She kept running. The ceiling collapsed above us. Water sloshed down in a torrent along with ruined furniture. Scaffolding tipped over and crashed. Water rained down on the plastic with a deafening roar. It didn't look like the renovations were going to get finished.

Mom ran around it and took the stairs toward the front door. I turned my head and I could see it.

The stairs broke through and I felt the world falling away under us. Mom kept running like she was using wings. She hit the front door and I felt it in my hip. We were outside. I was watching the house as mom ran across the lawn with us. The roof and top floor were gone. Water was blasting out of holes all around the sides like the house was bleeding. It didn't blow up. It just sort of folded in on itself like it was deflating.

Mom put us in the back of dad's car and started it. I didn't think she had the keys, so he must have left them inside. He was acting weird and distracted when he came in. Maybe he wasn't thinking about the keys.

He had been disconnected a lot since things had started getting bad in the house. Maybe mom was right that he had left us a long time ago. I had dealt with some of the same ghosts he had, so I knew how bad it could have been for him. I thought that maybe we should have tried to save him too.

As we pulled away, mom said, "I'm not sure where we are going yet, but we'll figure it out together. We may have to hide for a while, but we'll be okay. Everything will be okay. I promise."

Heather turned around in her seat and looked out the back window. I didn't look back toward the house.

Heather whispered, "Did you see him?"

I swallowed as I clicked my seatbelt. I thought I had. I wasn't sure if she had too. It would kill her, if she did. Heather would blame herself for us leaving dad behind. I wasn't sure, if when I saw him, he was still living or one of them.

I said, "What do you mean?"

"Do you think he was still in the house when we left?" she asked. "I wanted to see him one more time."

I stared at the back of my mother's head as she drove us away. I said, "Maybe one day."

After I said it, I wasn't sure if it was a promise or a threat.

Chapter 26
Foster Turner

I WRAPPED MY arms out around my bowl and brought a spoonful of the stew to my mouth. Most of the guys didn't take food from others, but it was still a force of habit to protect what was mine.

Uncle Duke sat down next to me. He had a skinny cigarette between his lips. The unlit tip bobbed up and down. I scanned the eyes of the other guys down the table from me to see if any of them were seeing it. Most were acting like they saw nothing most of the time anyway. Duke still preferred cigars, but he tended to pick up whatever he could grab. Sometimes he took toothpicks. He preferred it when we scraped together enough cash to go sit in a bar, but unlike him, I still had to eat.

The soup kitchens were good, but eventually they wanted to help a person get back on his feet. I had to move on then. Some of the churches had career centers. I would get on the computers when Duke wasn't looking and would search out details about where the girls might have gone. I hadn't found anything. My guess was that they changed their names. Wherever she had taken them, they had not been caught yet. I hoped it stayed that way. If they did get caught, my plan was to turn myself in and say it was all me. I hoped they were never found. I hoped the living never found them because I did not want the dead to know where they were either.

They had no idea what I was doing for them. Ruthie had no idea what I was giving up for her or the girls. I'm not sure whether they knew I was alive or not. It made me angry to imagine what she might be telling them about me. Things had gone bad, but that didn't make me a bad person. I didn't want my girls to remember me that way. Eventually, they would grow up only remembering what she told them about me. I had a bitter taste in the back of my throat I couldn't swallow away. I reached a hand out and touched her shoulder one last time, but she pulled away from me and then she was gone. The girls were gone.

"Penny for your thoughts," Duke said.

I ignored him.

The story had finally lost steam in the press , but it took a hell of a long time. It was still blamed on that Xandra woman. Her real name was Sylvia Parker and she had warrants for attempted murder and armed robbery in Florida. Police had caught her in Melinda Goshen's car. She had fought with police, but they took her in alive. She confessed to burning the trailer park, destroying the house, killing Goshen, and gathering the other remains found in there. Later, she said she did not remember confessing at all. Then, she stood up in court and confessed it all again, including killing me, Ruthie, and the girls. Later, she said she didn't even remember coming to court the day she confessed again.

I asked Duke about it and he just winked. Fortunately, he didn't know much about computers, so I could usually do my searches without him catching on.

As I finished my stew, Duke asked, "Where are we anyway?"

One of the guys looked up. Sometimes they could see the ghosts too. Sometimes just glimpses.

I said, "I don't know."

"Are we still in Charleston?" he asked.

"Just outside it, I think. A little up the coast."

"I could use a drink, kid. Let's go steal a wallet and get a drink."

"You mean you want to watch me drink, right?"

The others stood and moved their bowls farther down the table.

"I like to live vicariously through you," Duke said. "I saw your dad the other day."

"Shut up," I growled.

"The family is drifting. They are having trouble finding a place. They didn't take the time to lock into you the way I did. They stuck to the house, so they are adrift now instead of together like you and me."

"Lucky me," I said.

"Tell me the truth, Foster. Do you know where the girls are? If the family was back together, the others would have an easier time."

I shook my head. "That's why I don't want to know where they are."

"Shame," Duke said. "Sometimes we will walk past a spirit out on the street just standing and staring. They are lost and have no sense of time. It's a hell of a thing to die without a home. We need to go by one of those war cemeteries near Charleston. The ones that die in war have that same confused, lost thing going on. Kids that die before they have their identities fully established get the same thing. It's chilling. You should let me show you, so you know what's at stake here, Foster."

I dropped my spoon into my bowl and sat back. "I know what's at stake and I don't want them attached to you again. I'll drift forever after I die to have them free of you."

Duke snorted. "You'll see, Foster. You'll see. You're lucky you have me. I'll stick with you for the rest of your life and beyond. I promise."

I felt my throat go dry and found I wanted a stiff drink after all. I saw the other guys talking to the director and pointing at me. Talking to myself was getting me in trouble again.

I stood up and pushed my chair in. "We need to go, Uncle Duke."

I felt it in my knee and my back. Sleeping on cots and spending so much time outside in bad weather were playing hell on my body. I was a man of a certain age after all. The spot where the stitches in my chest had been itched, but I was pretty sure that part was all in my head. It was a phantom. Life was full of little things like that which haunted long after the physical manifestations were long gone. I flexed my hand and felt numbness in my fingers left over from the shaft of wood an ER doc had to remove from my forearm. I had to make a quick escape after that treatment too.

I saw the director and one of the pastors walking toward me. I licked my lips and turned toward the door. Slipping away was getting to be one of my greatest skills.

I walked toward the door so I wouldn't be grabbed and taken to the hospital for a psych evaluation. Duke followed me out the door onto the street. He always followed.

Armand Rosamilia is a New Jersey boy currently living in sunny Florida, where he writes when he's not sleeping. He's written over 100 stories that are currently available, including a few different series:
"Dying Days" extreme zombie series
  "Keyport Cthulhu" horror series
  "Flagler Beach Fiction Series" contemporary fiction
  "Metal Queens" non-fiction music series
       He also loves to talk in third person... because he's really that cool. He's a proud Active member of HWA as well.
       You can find The Arm N Toof's Dead Time Podcast at:
       https://www.facebook.com/ArmNToofDeadTime?fref=ts

       You can find him at http://armandrosamilia.com for not only his latest releases but interviews and guest posts with other authors he likes! Email him to talk about zombies, baseball and Metal: armandrosamilia@gmail.com

Jay Wilburn is an author of horror and speculative fiction that lives in coastal South Carolina near Myrtle Beach. He taught public school for sixteen years before becoming a full-time writer. He is currently working on a series of zombie novels based on the world of Dead Song. Each book will be accompanied by a soundtrack of songs recorded as if by the characters within the world of the novels.

Follow his many dark thoughts @AmongTheZombies on Twitter, the Jay Wilburn author page on Facebook, and at JayWilburn.com.

Jay Wilburn does video readings on his Patreon page at Patreon.com/JayWilburn

Zombie Fallout by Mark Tufo

Burkheart Witch Saga Set By Christine Sutton

The Hollowing By Travis Tufo

Chelsea Avenue By Armand Rosamilia

Thank you for reading The Enemy Held Near. Gaining exposure as independent authors relies mostly on word-of-mouth; please consider leaving a review wherever you purchased this story.